Geronimo Stilton

Thea Stilton
THE TREASURE
OF THE SEA

Scholastic Inc.

Library of Congress Cataloging-in-Publication data available

ISBN 978-1-338-03290-1

Text by Geronimo Stilton
Original title *Il segreto delle fate degli oceani*
Cover by Caterina Giorgetti (design) and Flavio Ferron (color)
Illustrations by Chiara Balleello and Barbara Pellizzari (design); Alessandro Muscillo (color)
Graphics by Marta Lorini

Special thanks to Tracey West
Translated by Emily Clement
Interior design by Becky James

10 9 8 7 6 5 4 3 2 1   16 17 18 19 20

Printed in China   62

First edition, October 2016

Thea Stilton and the Thea Sisters

THEA

PAULINA

Colette

Violet

nicky

PAMELA

The World of Aquamarina

Welcome to Aquamarina, the fantastic Land of the Sea! There are many beautiful, mysterious creatures in this truly special world. Come with us to find out who they are . . .

Queen Anemone lives in Pink Pearl Castle and rules her people with wisdom. She is the only creature in Aquamarina who can play the Sea Violin, a precious instrument that creates the magic that keeps the realm alive.

The Starry Soldiers protect the Pink Pearl Castle. These purple octopuses are grouchy, but are also brave and loyal.

The Fairies of the Deep are shy fairies who are healing experts. They are the custodians of the castle's Healing Room, which holds many cures and remedies.

The Eel of Ages is a mysterious, suspicious creature who lives in a remote part of the kingdom. She guards the Blue Pearl, which can answer any question asked of it.

 The Sea Nymphs live in a beautiful village filled with blooming gardens and pretty houses decorated with seashells. They are also wonderful cooks.

Captain Aragosa is the leader of the Black Claw Crew, a group of fierce pirate crustaceans who sail the seas on their ship, the *Claw of the Deep*.

 **The Cobalt Hermit Crab** is a great collector of seashells who lives at the Moving Dune. He has rude manners, but there's something very mysterious about him.

Esmeralda is the beautiful queen of the sirens. Her enchanting song can put anyone who hears it under her spell.

 Prince Nautilus had promised his heart to Queen Anemone. But just after he asked her to marry him, he disappeared.

WELCOME BACK, FRIENDS!

It was the end of summer, and five students gathered in a dorm room at Mouseford Academy. These mice called themselves the THEA SISTERS, after me, Thea Stilton. The six of us had gone on many **adventures** together.

On this afternoon, they were in Pam and Colette's room, talking about their summer VACATIONS. Pam was playing MUSIC on her laptop.

"Isn't this great?" she asked, turning down the sound. "I can't believe my brother Vince and I saw the **Cheddar Brothers Band** in Central Park. We don't get together much, but I love seeing him when I go back to **New York**!"

"What about you, Nicky?" asked Violet. "Did you have a good vacation?"

"It was really fun! I love going home to **AUSTRALIA**," the auburn-haired mouse replied. "I hiked and **CAMPED** for two weeks, sleeping out in the fresh air."

Colette looked shocked. "What, no **electricity**? How did you dry your fur?"

The Thea Sisters burst out *laughing*. They were all so different from one another, but that's why they were such good friends. *More than friends, actually . . . sisters!*

"The Australian wind is better than any **FUR DRYER**," Nicky replied. Then she held up her tablet to show a **PHOTO** of the Australian Outback. "Isn't it gorgeous?"

"**Holey cheese!** Next time I'm going with you!" cried Pam.

Nicky swiped to the next photo. "Check out this sunrise."

"Such beautiful colors," Violet said dreamily.

She looked up at the ceiling, where the Thea Sisters had painted a sky full of pink clouds after their return from our last magical adventure in the Land of Clouds.

The others followed her gaze, remembering that special world where beautiful fairies skillfully weave the clouds.

"It seems like it's been so long since our last mission for the SEVEN ROSES UNIT," Violet said.

"I wonder what other FANTASY WORLDS there are for us to explore?" Colette asked.

"I'm sure Will Mystery will contact us if he needs us," said Paulina, a little sadly.

Colette knew that Paulina and Will had a

special connection, and that her friend must be missing him.

"How was your visit home to **PERU**, Paulina?" Colette asked, hoping to distract her.

"**Fantastic!**" she cried, brightening up. "Actually, I almost forgot. I have presents for all of you."

She handed a **pink cotton pouch** to

each of her friends. "My little sister, Maria, made these for you."

Colette untied her pouch first and took out a beautiful beaded bracelet.

"Ooh, how pretty!" she said, putting it on her wrist. "I love it."

Pam showed off her RED bracelet. "Mine's awesome, too!"

Violet's was PURPLE and Nicky's was GREEN. And Maria had made one for Paulina in her sister's favorite color — ORANGE.

"Your little sister is such a sweetheart," said Nicky. "I hope she can come to visit us again soon."

"She even made one for THEA," Paulina said, holding up one more pouch.

"Speaking of Thea, it's strange that we

haven't seen her yet, isn't it?" remarked Nicky. "She came to **MOUSEFORD** yesterday for the journalism seminar."

"She must be very *busy*," Paulina guessed. "She usually has a lot to do to get ready for the seminar."

"Still, I hope we see her soon," said *Colette*. "Something *exciting* always happens when Thea comes to visit."

May I come in?

Just then, I tapped on the **HALF-OPEN DOOR**.

"Excuse me. May I come in?" I asked.

I knew I had a **worried expression** on my face, but I couldn't help it. Soon the Thea Sisters would find out why.

A NEW MISSION

"Thea! We were just talking about you!" Colette said, running to hug me.

I was **happy** to see my friends after a long vacation. But I had just spoken to Will Mystery, the director of the Seven Roses Unit, and I couldn't get his words out of my head.

"You seem worried, Thea," Violet said. "Is everything all right?"

"Actually, I'm not sure," I replied.

"NEWS FROM WILL?" Paulina asked.

I nodded. Nicky quickly closed the door. Any communication about the Seven Roses Unit had to remain a **SECRET**.

"I received a mysterious phone call from Will," I began.

"What did he say?" Nicky asked.

"He couldn't tell me much, because he's still doing research," I explained. "But there's a **problem** on the Living Map. It looks like another FANTASY WORLD is in danger."

"Does he need our help?" asked Pam, eager to begin a **NEW MISSION**.

THE SEVEN ROSES UNIT

The Seven Roses Unit is a supersecret research center that studies fantasy worlds. These lands contain characters from legends and fables.

LIVING MAP

Inside the Hall of the Seven Roses is a Living Map that depicts the fantasy worlds. It shows the condition of each world and can signal danger.

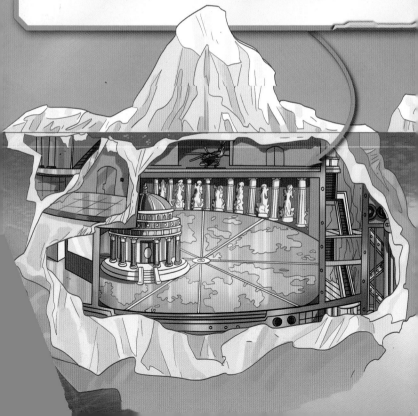

CRYSTAL PENDANTS

Anyone wishing to enter any room in the unit must wear their special rose-shaped crystal pendant. It contains their personal information and clearance levels.

CRYSTAL ELEVATOR

This elevator made of crystal is a portal that can take passengers to the fantasy worlds. It is activated by playing a keyboard, and only Will Mystery knows the tune that will make it work.

"He does," I answered. "He asked us to join him as **soon** as possible at the headquarters of the Seven Roses Unit."

"Hooray!" cheered the Thea Sisters.

Normally I applaud the enthusiasm of these young rodents, but they were forgetting to be **careful**.

"Not so loud," I reminded them. "Someone will hear us."

Hooray!

Let's go!

Not so loud!

"**Sorry**, Thea," Nicky apologized. "We got carried away."

"When are we leaving?" Colette asked.

I looked out the window. It was almost **sunset**.

"Will is sending a

helicopter for us at six tomorrow morning," I told them. "That way we can leave without drawing too much **ATTENTION**."

"Perfect, Thea!" said Pam. "We'll be right on time. I'll make sure Colette wakes up extra early to get her packing done."

"I should be insulted, but I know you're right!" Colette said with a laugh.

"Good," I said. "Just remember to keep this mission a **SECRET**."

"We will!" the five friends promised.

I turned to leave, but Paulina stopped me.

"Thea, wait," she said, holding out a **fabric pouch**. "This is for you. My sister made one for each of us."

"Thank you," I said, and opened the pouch to find a beautiful bracelet with beads in every color of the **rainbow**. "I love it!"

I went back to my office and checked for any **messages** from Will — but there were none. I frowned. Will had sounded so **SERIOUS** on the phone. I hoped that we wouldn't be *too late* to save the fantasy world in danger.

Since I didn't know where we were going, I only packed my **BACKPACK** with necessities: my tablet, my laptop, a flashlight, and a notebook and pen. If any *special clothing* was required, I was sure Will would have us covered.

Then I tried to get some sleep. The next day would be a long one.

IT WAS THE BEGINNING OF A NEW ADVENTURE!

SUPERSONIC TRAVEL

The next morning, I woke up before sunrise. I felt **wide awake**. I couldn't wait to get to the Seven Roses Unit!

I **quickly** made my way through the empty hallways of Mouseford Academy, then crossed the garden and headed for the **heliport** by the shore.

The Thea Sisters were already there and waiting for me. I could see they were just as **EXCITED** as I was to start our new adventure!

Pam pointed to the sky. "**LOOK, it's coming!**"

We could see the **RED** helicopter flying across the **BLUE** sky.

The **helicopter** landed on the field in

front of us. The **special agent** at the controls motioned for us to get on board.

We quickly boarded and fastened our seat belts. The pilot handed each of us a headset with a CRYSTAL visor.

"Wear these, please," he instructed. "They're a **prototype** of a new communication device."

"What kind of communication?" Nicky asked, but before he could answer each visor projected a HOLOGRAPHIC IMAGE of Will Mystery!

"Hello, Thea!" he said. "Hello, Paulina, Pam, Nicky, Violet, and Colette!"

We all greeted him.

"It's quite a **SURPRISE** to see you like this," I said.

"I thought this helicopter ride would be a good **test** for the new headsets," he said. "What do you think?"

Cool technology!

"You **sound** great!" said Colette.

"And you **LOOK** great,

too!" Paulina said. Then she blushed. "You know what I mean. We can SEE YOU well."

Will smiled. "Good to know! Have a nice trip. I'll be here waiting for you."

His image VANISHED, leaving us with a thousand questions about the mission ahead. But those answers would have to wait. We settled in as the helicopter flew toward ICY ANTARCTICA at supersonic speed.

An Eventful
Arrival

The state-of-the-art helicopter swiftly and silently carried us to the headquarters of the **SEVEN ROSES UNIT**.

Shortly after Will signed off, we spotted the tip of a **HUGE ICEBERG** on the horizon, where the secret entrance to headquarters was located. The pilot was preparing to land when a **GUST OF WIND** jolted the helicopter.

"What's happening?" Violet cried.

Then a **SECOND GUST OF WIND** shook the aircraft. This time, the pilot was ready for it and kept the helicopter as **STEADY** as he could.

"There's a freezing current colliding

with a **warm** one," he replied through the headset. "Just hold tight and stay calm."

The pilot began the **descent**, slowly circling the iceberg. With each **spiral**, the helicopter flew lower and lower. We were **hovering** just above the ice when he pushed a button on the control panel. The **ICEBERG** split in two, and the pilot guided the aircraft down into the crevice.

We **slowly** moved down through a large **tunnel** of ice.

Paulina gazed out the window. "Each time we do this, I'm **amazed**," she said.

"I know," agreed Colette. "Just think: We're heading into the **depths** of the ocean!"

The helicopter came to a stop on the arrival platform. Will was standing there waiting for us.

"**Welcome!**" he greeted us. "How was your trip?"

"Well, we did experience some turbulence up there," Violet said, shivering at the memory.

Let's get to work!

"But the pilot handled it very well," added Nicky.

"I don't doubt it," Will said, and he **saluted** the special agent in the cockpit. Then he turned to me and the Thea Sisters.

"You're probably **wondering** why I called you here so quickly," he said. "As Thea has told you, I have reason to believe that one of the FANTASY WORLDS is in trouble. There is a disturbance on the Living Map."

"Which **world** are you talking about?" I asked anxiously. So far, we had met all kinds of fairies and magical creatures — everything from fairies of Japanese legends to a PRINCE from the lost city of Atlantis.

"Follow me to the Hall of the Seven Roses, and I'll explain everything," he replied. "But we must hurry!"

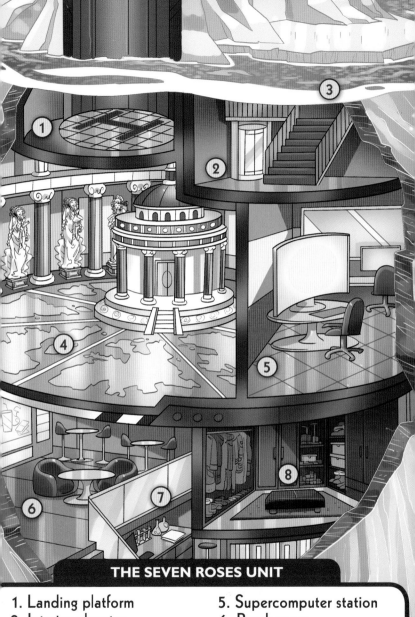

THE SEVEN ROSES UNIT

1. Landing platform
2. Interior elevator
3. Access to the iceberg
4. Hall of the Seven Roses
5. Supercomputer station
6. Break room
7. Research laboratory
8. Wardrobe storage room

A DIFFICULT CASE

We followed Will to the **HALL OF THE SEVEN ROSES**, where we were surprised to find another **special agent** waiting for us. He was a **BLUE-EYED**, bearded rodent. The color of his hoodie matched his eyes, and on the front was the **symbol** of the Seven Roses, also in blue.

"This is **JACK**, who is in charge of the Undersea Research Lab," Will said.

"**Nice to meet you, Jack**," I said, shaking his

Nice to meet you!

Hi, Thea!

paw. "I'm Thea Stilton, and these are my students, Paulina, Pam, Nicky, Colette, and Violet."

"I didn't know that the unit had an **Undersea Research Lab**," Paulina said.

Will nodded. "We called in Jack because there is **something wrong** in one of our undersea worlds."

The mouselets and I exchanged worried looks.

"Take a look at the **Living Map** and you'll understand," Will continued, and we followed him once more.

The huge map was **ETCHED** all across the floor of the hall. Will stopped at a part of the map showing **SWIRLS** and water currents. A large **CRACK** ran through the area, which bore the name . . .

Aquamarina, the Land of the Sea

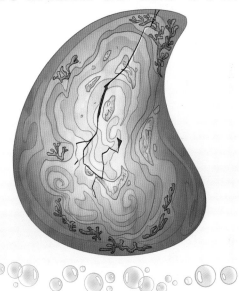

"**Aquamarina**," read Colette.

"What a lovely name," said Violet.

"It's a magnificent world, from what we know," added Jack. "There are creatures there that can't be found anywhere else."

"We must find out what caused this **CRACK**, and save the realm," Will concluded.

"Do you have any idea what the **problem** might be?" asked Paulina.

Jack nodded. "We have discovered something: We can no longer hear the *Music of the Sea*. It is the magic that powers everything in Aquamarina."

"Without it, the land will **not exist** much longer," Will said sadly.

"Ever since the music stopped, the fish have been losing their **BEAUTIFUL COLORS**," Jack continued. "Soon they may disappear altogether."

"How sad!" said Violet.

"It would be **very sad** to lose this land and all of the wonders in it," Will agreed. "Which is why we must travel there and find out why the *music* has stopped."

"You know you can count on us," I assured him.

"**Yes, you can!**"
echoed the Thea Sisters.

"Thank you," Will said.
"Here's the PLAN.
Jack will remain here at
headquarters and follow us
via computer. We'll be using a new
GPS system to orient ourselves. Once we're
back, he can download our data and archive
all the information we've discovered."

He held up the GPS, a small black box
with a screen. "This new version has a
sensitive data collection system, and it can
store an **ENORMOUSE** amount of data
besides."

"I'm EXCITED to see you test it out," said
Jack. "Right now we only have a limited
amount of information about Aquamarina in
our system."

"I'm curious," said Paulina. "How will we get around in an underwater world? A **SUBMARINE**?"

"Or with diving gear?" I asked. "We may need to bring reserve tanks of oxygen."

Will smiled. "Don't worry, Thea. We won't need oxygen."

How will we breathe?

You'll see!

"Are you sure? How can that be?" I asked, surprised.

"Like all fantasy worlds, Aquamarina has a magical environment," he explained. "Once we're within its borders, we will be able to breathe normally, just like we do here."

"We'll be just like **fish**!" said Violet.

"Speaking of fish, are we going to **EAT** before we leave?" asked Pam. "I'm so **hungry** I could eat a peanut-butter-and-jellyfish sandwich!"

"Also, we really should check the **supercomputer** before we leave," said Paulina. "Like we do before each mission."

"I was just going to suggest that," said Will. "Let's go."

We all headed to the supercomputer station, where we could read all the data gathered so far about

Aquamarina.

AQUAMARINA

POPULATION: Ocean fairies and aquatic creatures

LEGEND: According to legend, the ocean fairies produce sweet music, the *MUSIC OF THE SEA*, which grants good health and harmony to all of the realm's creatures, and keeps the magical land alive.

RULER: Queen Anemone, a fairy of great beauty and courage, rules Aquamarina and keeps harmony in the realm with the help of the fairies of her court. They are the **CLEARWATER FAIRIES; FAIRIES OF THE COLD SEA; FAIRIES OF THE WARM SEA; WATER CURRENT FAIRIES;** and **FAIRIES OF THE DEEP**.

HOW TO REACH AQUAMARINA:

The entrance is located in the mysterious **TURQUOISE GROTTO**. To enter, you must hold your breath and close your eyes.

PINK PEARL CASTLE:

The marvelous dwelling of the fairies is located in the middle of Placid Lagoon. It is defended by a **CORAL WALL** made of stinging coral that closes off the castle when unexpected guests arrive.

HOW TO REACH THE CASTLE:

Follow the **DIAMOND CURRENT**, lit by the shimmering reflections around it.

SUIT UP!

I carefully studied the data about the ocean fairies provided by the supercomputer. Will had told us that we wouldn't need oxygen to breathe underwater, but I still had some questions for him.

"It says that the **Pink Pearl Castle** is guarded by a stinging coral barrier," I told Will. "It sounds like we will need to wear some protective clothing. Maybe a wet suit?"

Will nodded. "Certainly, Thea. A wet suit will provide protection from the stinging coral of the **coral wall**, and also from cold currents and other dangers that we might encounter in Aquamarina."

"Do you have **wet suits** for us?" asked Paulina.

"Not just any wet suits," Will replied. "Ever since the crack in Aquamarina appeared, our lab has been working on creating special wet suits using the latest technology."

"Cool! Can we see them?" Pam asked.

"Follow me," Will said, and he led us down another hallway to a large **STEEL DOOR**.

To enter, Will lined up his right eye with a sensor next to the door, and then tapped in a code on a keyboard. The door slid open.

We were squeakless!

Follow me!

Inside the room were six large glass display cases. Each case contained a sleek white wet suit with colorful trim.

"These might be protective, but they look like high fashion to me," Colette said.

Jack grinned. "That's just a plus. Each one is made of a specially engineered material that will keep you warm in cold water. And each suit contains a camera and computer chip, so you'll be able to collect data wherever you go."

I smiled at Will. "You've thought of everything!"

"They're all ready for you," he replied. "To get them, you each just need to take your rose-shaped CRYSTAL PENDANT and place it up against the display case sensor. Push the **red button**, and the

display case will open."

"Okay, we're ready!" the Thea Sisters responded.

Will gave us each our pink crystal pendants, which contained our personal information and gave us access to the most **SECRET** places in the Seven Roses Unit. Then he and Jack left the room.

For a moment, we all **STARED** at the cases that contained the wet suits.

"Did you notice that each one has a *different color* trim?" Colette asked.

"We should each pick our favorite color," Nicky suggested. "Colette, I know you're choosing the **FUCHSIA**."

"Of course!" Colette cried.

"I'd like the **PURPLE**, please," said Violet.

Pam chose **RED**, Nicky chose **GREEN**, and Paulina chose **ORANGE**.

I walked to the case with the **blue wet suit**, placed my pendant in front of the sensor, and pressed the **red button**. The case sprang open! The others did the same, and soon we each held our wet suit.

Super!

Beautiful!

So chic!

Let's put them on!

Wow!

THE TURQUOISE GROTTO

We put on our **special wet suits** and then joined Will and Jack outside the room.

"Let's get to the crystal elevator," Will said, hurrying down the hall. "It will take us to a place called the Turquoise Grotto. It's the passageway to Aquamarina."

"A grotto is a cave, right?" asked Nicky. "There's a **beautiful** one back home in Australia, right on the beach."

"I think you'll find that this one is beautiful, too," Will promised.

When we boarded the crystal elevator, Jack waved to us as the door closed.

"**Safe travels!**" he called out.

Then we heard music in the elevator,

and it sped toward our destination.

"This music is so **relaxing** . . . almost like a *lullaby*," remarked Violet.

"It's inspired by the *Music of the Sea*," Will told us.

"You mean the music that is missing?" Nicky asked, and Will nodded.

Pam gasped. "We can't let such a beautiful MELODY disappear!"

Soon the elevator stopped, and the

What sweet music!

doors opened. The sight in front of us left us squeakless once again. The Turquoise Grotto was a **CAVE** with a high ceiling. The walls above us twinkled with a magical **BLUE SPARKLE** that reflected on the surface of the water.

Wow!

It's a cave!

Those sparkles...

Where is the passage?

Underwate...

Colette gazed up at the ceiling. "Those SPARKLY things look like jewels!"

"They look like animals to me," Nicky observed.

"They're mollusks," Will explained. "They eat a blue plankton that glows in the dark, and it turns them blue."

"I hope I remember this, so I can PAINT it," Violet said.

"How do we get to Aquamarina from here?" Paulina asked.

Will pointed to the water. "We have to dive down, and then follow the LIGHT."

We leaned forward and saw something **glowing** beneath the surface of the water.

"We have to **swim** down there?" Colette asked.

"Yes, there's a **tunnel** in the rock, beneath the **waterline**, that leads to Aquamarina," Will replied. "Hold your breath until we reach the tunnel. Then we'll

be able to **breathe** freely. I'll go first —
follow me."

We each **held our breath** and
dove in, one after another, trusting that what
we knew about this **magical** place was
correct.

We swam through a **ROCKY TUNNEL** —
and then the **secret world** of Aquamarina
appeared before our eyes.

WELCOME TO AQUAMARINA!

"Are we all here? Is everyone okay?" Will asked as soon as we exited the **tunnel**.

"Yes, all okay, thanks," we replied.

Colette looked surprised. "Hey, we can talk underwater!"

"It's part of the magic of Aquamarina," Will said.

"FANTASY WORLDS are truly unique places," I added.

We can talk!

Paulina looked around. "Now we have to find the

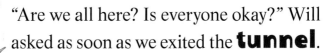

DIAMOND CURRENT

that the supercomputer was talking about."

"What's that up there?" Nicky asked, pointing.

Right in front of us was what looked like a shining path in the water that snaked and moved like a river.

"Cheese and crackers! That's got to be the *DIAMOND CURRENT*!" exclaimed Pam.

Colette swam closer. "Look, there are shiny little bits in the current, making it sparkle. They look like diamonds!"

"They're actually tiny living organisms that are carried by the current," explained Will.

I swam into the current, eager to get

to the Pink Pearl Castle. The others followed me. As we headed along the sparkly path, we observed the wonders of Aquamarina.

"There are plants and creatures of all SHAPES and COLORS here!" Colette gushed.

Suddenly, Nicky cried out, "Look over there, at those fish! The color has started to FADE from their scales."

They're losing their colors . . .

"It's happening to the **tentacles** of this anemone, too," said Paulina, pointing to a creature in front of her.

Will frowned. "THE SITUATION IS EVEN MORE SERIOUS

THAN WE THOUGHT," he said. "So many creatures are **LOSING** their colors!"

"Without the *Music of the Sea*, the magic of this land is fading," I said. "We must find out what happened, and we must do it **SOON** . . . or this enchanted world will be erased **FOREVER**!"

We swam *FASTER*, continuing to follow the Diamond Current.

Then, in the distance, we spotted an **enormouse underwater plant**.

"That looks like bushes made of cotton candy!" Pam remarked.

CuRiouS, we moved closer . . .

THE GIANT STICKY SPONGE

"I don't think it's cotton candy. It looks like a **GIANT SEA SPONGE**," Paulina said.

"It's too *pretty* to be a sponge," Colette said, swimming closer. "It looks like lovely *ruffled* fabric!"

"Don't get too close, Colette," Will warned. "We don't know what it is, and it could be **DANGEROUS** to us."

"How could something so beautiful be dangerous?" Colette asked. "See? There are *glittering specks* all throughout it."

Paulina swam up to her and tried to pull her back. "Colette, we have to be careful."

"I will — but I have to get a CLOSER LOOK," Colette said. "Who knows when I'll see anything like this again?"

She swam right up to the sponge. We watched anxiously as she examined the strange plant.

"It looks so soft," she said. "I would love to make a dress out of this!"

She REACHED OUT with one of her paws to touch it.

Suddenly, a thick yellow foam sprayed out of the sponge. It stuck to Colette's paws!

Will immediately swam

It looks so soft . . .

over to her, but the foam had already spread, surrounding poor Colette.

"THE FOAM IS GROWING BIGGER!"

Nicky shouted with alarm.

"Quick! Let's help her!" Paulina cried, and Pam, Nicky, and I swam over to Will. Paulina and Violet hung back, frightened.

"It's like the sponge is trying to TRAP Colette," Paulina remarked.

"She'll be a prisoner down here forever!" wailed Violet.

"Stay calm," Will advised them. "Her special wet suit will PRotect her for a while. But we have to try to get her loose."

The foam was spreading out even farther now, trying to reach me and the others.

"HELP! HELP ME!"

Colette shouted, struggling to free herself from her sticky, wet prison.

"Colette, **DON'T MOVE**," Will warned. "The more you move, the faster the foam will grow. Hang on and we'll try to free you."

He reached out his arm to grab her, but a cloud of foam stopped him.

"Will! Look out!" I yelled.

I instinctively moved toward him to help, but the STICKY FOAM quickly surrounded me. NOW I WAS TRAPPED, TOO!

PURPLE INK TO THE RESCUE

The **GIANT SPONGE** had imprisoned us in its foamy trap! After me, Nicky and Pam got **STUCK**.

Even though Will had warned us not to **move**, we tried to pull ourselves away from the foam. But **more and more** foam kept coming. Soon it would reach Paulina and Violet, who had stayed behind us.

And if that wasn't enough, I could no longer see the **DIAMOND CURRENT**, which was our only hope of finding Pink Pearl Castle!

"**THEA, GIVE ME YOUR PAW!**" Will called out, reaching for me.

I saw that he had managed to grab Colette's

paw before the foam had completely surrounded her.

I yanked one arm out of the foam and reached, **stretching** with all my might. I found Will's paw, and that gave me COURAGE. So I reached out and grabbed Nicky's paw, and she reached for Violet.

We were safe — but for how long?

"The foam is PULLING me in!" Colette

I can't see anyone!

I'm right here!

Heeelp!

cried. "I can't hold on!"

Then I heard Nicky shout. "**Thea, look!**"

A strange, **DARK SUBSTANCE** that looked like purple ink was heading toward us. The liquid **FLOATED** right to us and mixed with the **foam**.

"What is this stuff?" Colette asked.

"I don't know, but it's **attacking** the sticky foam!" Will replied.

Hey! I'm trying! Take my paw, Thea! Help me!

It was true. The purple liquid was MELTING the foam on contact!

"Holey cheese! We're saved!" Pam cheered.

As soon as we were free, we swam away from the sponges.

"This PURPLE INK is amazing," Paulina said, studying the remnants on her wet suit. "It completely dissolved the foam!"

"But where did it come from?" Colette asked, looking around.

"Maybe from them!" Nicky said, pointing to two creatures swimming toward us. They looked like **purple octopuses**, and they each had long arms.

"They don't seem very friendly," Paulina observed.

She was right. The octopuses were frowning severely.

They swam right up to us.

"Stay where you are, strangers!" one of them ordered in a commanding voice.

"Let's do as he says," I told the others. "Even if we wanted to, we couldn't *ESCAPE*."

So we **STOPPED** in our tracks, waiting to see what these octopuses wanted with us.

"Who are you? What are you doing in **Aquamarina**?" the first octopus asked.

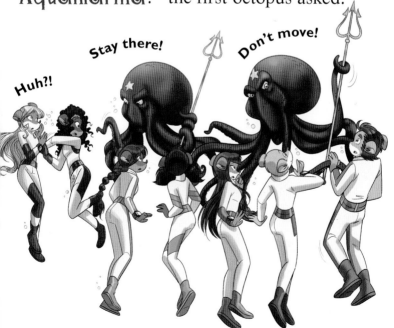

"We're here because we know that Aquamarina is in **SERIOUS DANGER**, and we want to help you," Will replied.

The creatures shared a curious look. Then the one who was doing the talking continued.

"Do you have **permission** to enter our realm?" he asked.

"Well, you see —" Will started to explain, but the other octopus gave an **impatient** growl.

"**Seize them!**" he commanded.

The two octopuses reached out with their long arms. One of them lashed around Pam.

Let go!

"**LET GO!**" she squeaked.

One by one their LONG ARMS wrapped around us.

"Who are you, and why are you doing this?" I asked.

"We're the STARRY SOLDIERS, THE GUARDIANS OF PINK PEARL CASTLE," replied the guard who had grabbed me. "We have orders to arrest all intruders."

"We're not **intruders**!" Paulina protested.

"We'll see about that," the octopus said. "Now come with us to the **Pink Pearl Castle**."

Then it hit us: *That was exactly where we wanted to go!*

Will turned to the one who seemed to be in charge. "We won't resist. You can let go of us."

"Why should we **TRUST YOU**?" the leader asked.

"We give you our word," Will promised.

The creature's eyes narrowed. "Very well," he said. "We will let go of you. But I'm warning you: **NO GAMES**, or you'll be sorry!"

"That won't happen," Will said.

The Starry Soldiers released their arms and we **stretched**, glad to be free. Then

we swam with them across a sandbar, **algae patches**, and rocky boulders.

Any fish we passed moved aside in **FEAR** when they saw the octopuses. Soon, the guards slowed down, and we saw a **wondrous** sight in front of us.

A bright red **coral reef** stretched out across the bottom of the ocean floor, leading right to . . . THE MAJESTIC PINK PEARL CASTLE!

INSIDE THE CORAL REEF

"Is that the **coral wall** that protects the castle?" asked Violet, pointing to the reef.

"It is," answered one of the guards. "It is **IMPOSSIBLE** to pass, unless you enter through the gate."

"Come!" barked the other. "We are almost there."

The guards led us to an **imposing** gate made of twisted red coral. At the top was the symbol of Pink Pearl Castle: two sea horses facing each other in a circle of coral.

One of the octopuses produced a **golden key** with a seashell-shaped handle.

"The passage leading to the castle is very **NARROW** and lined with **STINGING CORAL**," he said, turning to look at us. "All members of the queen's court may pass through unharmed. But you must be very CAREFUL."

"The coral stings are very painful," added the other guard. "It can be deadly."

"DEADLY?" asked Colette worriedly.

"Our wet suits should **protect** us," Will said. "But they have never been tested with this stinging coral. Try to swim very cautiously."

"Are you sure there isn't **another** entrance?" asked Pam. "Like, maybe where the pizza delivery guy comes in?"

"This is the only way," the guard said, his voice **deep** and **serious**.

"We'll be all right," I assured everyone. "Just be very careful."

The guard unlocked the gate with the **key** and it swung open. The passageway really was narrow, and **SPIKES** of coral jutted out on either side.

The guard **swam** through, and I **swam** after him, followed by Colette, Nicky, Violet, Pam, Paulina, and Will. The other octopus closed out the line and the doors of the **coral gate** closed behind us with a quiet click.

Our octopus guide *effortlessly* swam between the protruding coral, but it was not so easy for us mice. The coral seemed to be reaching out for us with long, sharp, **THREATENING** branches.

"How's everyone doing?" I asked, looking behind me.

"Doing okay, Thea," Colette replied. "But I can't wait to get to the end of this!"

"And I'm doing — **WHOA**!" Pam cried.

"What's wrong?" Will asked.

"I accidentally brushed against the coral," she replied.

"Oh no, Pam! Are you okay?" Violet asked.

"My wet suit protected me, but still, it felt pretty **sharp**," Pam reported.

"Stay focused, everyone!" I warned.

We swam farther through the passage.

"I can feel a *STRONG CURRENT* coming up!" Will suddenly called out in warning.

Just as he said it, the current **pushed** against us. I steadied myself, but I looked behind me and saw the current slamming into Paulina! She TUMBLED right into a patch of **prickly coral**.

"Ow!" she yelled.

Will was the closest to her, and he immediately swam to her side. He pulled her away from the coral, but her eyes were closed and her body was limp. He held her in his arms.

"Look!" Violet cried. "Her wet suit has been **TORN** by the coral!"

The octopus behind Will swam up to him and **frowned**.

"What's happened to her?" Will asked.

"She was **STUNG** by the coral," replied the guard. "Those who are stung fall into a **deep sleep**."

"Oh no!" cried Colette.

"How do we **wake her** up?" Nicky asked.

"We must bring her to the castle," said the octopus. "She can be **healed** there."

I looked at Paulina's still face. The poor mouselet was not moving at all.

"**LET'S HURRY!**" I urged.

73

The lead octopus guided us through the last NARROW STRETCH of the coral tunnel. We swam into the warm, calm water of the Placid Lagoon.

The castle was right in front of us. Will HURRIED toward the entrance, still carrying Paulina.

"I hope the fairies can help Paulina!" said Colette, holding back tears.

AT PiNK PEARL CASTLE

Polished **pink shells** covered the tall front doors of Pink Pearl Castle. The Starry Soldiers knocked as soon as we reached them.

The doors opened, and we walked into an **ENORMOUSE** hall. Columns of twisted **LiLAC** coral supported the high ceiling.

"It's so *beautiful!*" murmured Violet.

The guards led us down the corridor.

We're here!

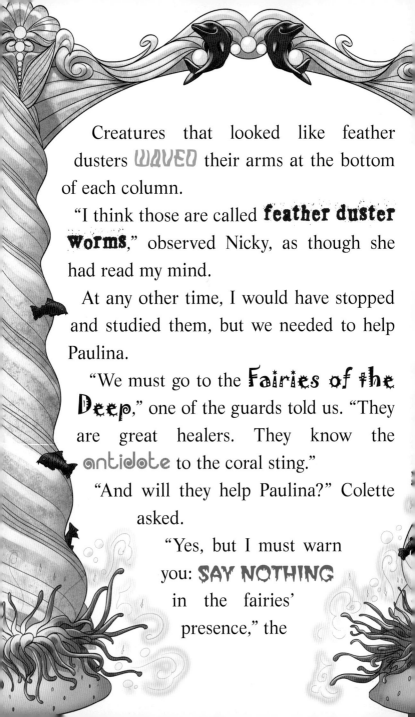

Creatures that looked like feather dusters WAVED their arms at the bottom of each column.

"I think those are called **feather duster worms**," observed Nicky, as though she had read my mind.

At any other time, I would have stopped and studied them, but we needed to help Paulina.

"We must go to the **Fairies of the Deep**," one of the guards told us. "They are great healers. They know the antidote to the coral sting."

"And will they help Paulina?" Colette asked.

"Yes, but I must warn you: **SAY NOTHING** in the fairies' presence," the guard replied. "They are very **shy** and do not like strangers."

"Let us do the TALKING," added the other octopus.

"We'll do whatever you say!" Pam promised.

We continued along the hallway, and then headed **down** a staircase into another corridor. Suddenly, the water became much colder.

"The Fairies of the Deep live in this wing of the castle," the guard explained.

Colette shivered. "It's chilly down here. And the light is much dimmer."

"The Fairies of the Deep don't like LIGHT," the other

octopus said. "They are very shy, as I told you."

At that moment a figure came moving toward us: a tall, slender fairy with **black hair** and beautiful **amethyst** eyes.

An octopus swam forward and bowed. "Good day, kind Cora," he said. "Please pardon the **intrusion**, but these strangers have urgent need of your help."

Cora looked alarmed. "**Strangers?** Here, at Pink Pearl Castle?"

Then she noticed Paulina, who was still in Will's arms.

"**What happened?**" the fairy asked. She had an amazing voice. It sounded like it was coming from the **deepest depths** of the ocean.

"She was **INJURED** by a branch from the coral wall," replied the guard.

"Can you help her?" Violet blurted out.

Violet had ignored the **WARNING** of the octopuses, and the Fairy of the Deep's eyes turned as **HARD AS STONE**. But luckily for us, her gaze soon softened.

"Bring her to the Healing Room," she said.

She turned and led us to a small circular room. Shelves covered the walls, each one filled with dozens of jars of healing herbs and potions.

FOR BURNS AND VENOMOUS SCRATCHES

A fairy with dark blue hair swam into the room and motioned for us to leave. Our hearts were full of both fear for Paulina and hope that she would be okay. But we left her in the care of the fairies.

THE TALE OF THE FAIRIES

We waited and waited for the fairies to emerge from the Healing Room with Paulina.

"What's happening in there?" asked Nicky anxiously. "I'm going to go check."

Will took her by the arm. "We must have faith in the fairies. And above all, we must not disturb them!"

"Could we at least knock?" Violet asked.

"Will is right," I said. "Let's allow the fairies to do what they do best."

Finally, the door opened, and Cora motioned for us to come in.

"She's awake!" Violet cried.

Paulina was seated inside a giant seashell, on top of a soft bed of algae.

"How do you feel?" Colette asked, gently hugging her.

"Not too bad," she replied. "I just have a little headache."

"That is caused by the coral's venom. It will pass quickly," Cora said.

I turned to her. "How can we thank you?"

"The credit also belongs to my sister, Phylla," she said, pointing to the blue-haired fairy. "And also the castle guards. If they hadn't brought her to us so quickly, we could not have healed her."

"Thank you, Starry Soldiers!" cheered the Thea Sisters.

"You gave us a good scare," Will said, squeezing Paulina's paw. "I was so worried about you."

She smiled. "I was trying to be careful, but that current was too strong!"

"Is Paulina well enough to continue our mission?" I asked Cora.

She nodded. "Yes, but she must be careful not to bump into the coral again. Our healing herbs won't have the same effect a second time."

"I will be **careful**," Paulina promised.

"Thank you, Cora and Phylla."

The fairy nodded. "I can see that your hearts are GENEROUS and good. Guards, let them go as they please."

The two Starry Soldiers swam away, and Will approached the fairies.

"We thank you for your kindness, Fairies of the Deep," he said. "But before we go, if we may be so bold, we have another favor to ask you."

"You may speak," Cora said.

"We would like to see Queen Anemone," said Will.

The two fairies exchanged a concerned look.

"That may be difficult," said Phylla.

"Why?" I asked.

"It is a COMPLICATED time in the kingdom," she said.

"And the queen is suffering," added Cora.

"Because of the problems in Aquamarina?" I asked.

"Yes, but the queen also **suffers** because her heart is sad," said Cora.

"What happened to her?" asked Pam.

"The queen was always a JOYFUL fairy with a good heart," the fairy answered. "Her happiness was complete when she met **Nautilus**, a prince with a heart as good as her own."

"The two fell in **love**," continued Phylla. "And Prince Nautilus asked the queen to marry him."

"*Did she say yes?*" asked Pam.

"She did, but their happiness did not last long," replied the fairy. "A few days later, the prince disappeared without a trace!"

"Nobody knows what happened to him?"

asked Paulina. "How can that be?"

"The queen has heard nothing from her beloved prince," Phylla answered. "She does not know if his heart changed, or if some **terrible fate** has befallen him."

"Oh, how tragic!" said Violet.

"Please, may we speak to her?" I asked.

Anemone, I offer you my heart . . .

And I accept!

Cora nodded. "We will ask her if she will see you. But we cannot promise anything."

We followed the two fairies back down the corridor. The STARRY SOLDIERS rejoined us, and we headed toward the castle entrance.

We soon stopped in front of a majestic door made of pink coral and adorned with shining pearls.

"The Royal Apartments are behind this door," said Phylla.

"Wait here for us," said Cora, and the two of them entered the queen's chamber.

They returned a few minutes later, looking happy. It was the first time we had seen them smile since we had met them.

"The queen has agreed to meet with you, but only for a few minutes," reported Cora.

"Thank you, kind fairies," I said, and then we followed them to see the queen.

QUEEN ANEMONE

We found Queen Anemone seated on a marvelous seashell-shaped throne. She was beautiful, with turquoise eyes and long green hair. She wore a crown adorned with shimmering pearls. On either side of her stood a fairy attendant.

The sadness on the queen's face was plain to see. She motioned for us to come forward.

"I am Anemone, Ruler of Aquamarina," she said. "What brings you to Pink Pearl Castle? You must be from some far-off land."

"Correct, Your Majesty," said Will, with a bow. "Thank you for meeting with us. My name is Will Mystery. I research fantasy worlds. I saw that your kingdom was in

DANGER, and my companions and I **HURRIED** here to offer you our help."

The queen nodded. "The **Fairies of the Deep** told me this. But they did not tell me how you knew of our trouble."

"It would take a long time to explain, and we must work quickly to save your land,"

I am Anemone, Ruler of Aquamarina!

Will explained. "We noticed that the **COLORS** of some of your sea creatures have started to fade."

The queen nodded sorrowfully. "Yes. It is **BREAKING** my heart."

"Is it because the Music of the Sea is gone?" asked Colette.

The queen raised an eyebrow. "And how do you know about that?"

"We have advanced instruments at our research center," replied Will. "Could you tell us what you know about the music?"

The queen got a faraway look in her eyes. "This land was created when the first note of the Music of the Sea was first played," she said. "The music and the land are one. Without the music, this realm — and everything in it — will FADE AWAY forever."

"That's **terrible**!" cried Colette. "What happened to the music?"

"The Music of the Sea is produced by a very ancient instrument, the **Sea Violin**," Queen Anemone explained. "The body of the violin is made out of a seashell, and the strings are silk and **golden wire**."

"It must make a **beautiful** sound," said Violet, who played violin herself.

"Beautiful and **unique**," said the queen. "I used to play the Sea Violin every night, to bring **HARMONY** to Aquamarina and keep the realm alive."

"But what is keeping you from playing it now?" I asked.

The queen's face **DARKENED**. "The Sea

Violin is gone. It was **STOLEN** from me."

We were squeakless.

"My guards have **SEARCHED** for it far and wide, but they have not found it," the queen said sadly.

"Do you have any idea who could have **STOLEN** it?" Will asked.

Queen Anemone shook her head. "All of my subjects know how **IMPORTANT** the music is. Why would any of them want to steal it?"

"There must be someone who knows something about it!" I said.

"There is one creature who can come to our aid," said the queen. "The Eel of Ages. She is a giant moray eel, and the wisest creature in the ocean. She knows the most deeply **HIDDEN SECRETS** of Aquamarina."

"What makes her so wise?" Paulina asked.

"Only she can consult the *Blue Pearl*,"

answered the queen. "This gem contains all the knowledge of Aquamarina."

"If this eel is the **only** creature who can find out where the Sea Violin is, why haven't you asked her yet?" said Will.

The queen sighed. "Unfortunately, we can't. The Eel of Ages lives in a cave located beyond the **INFINITE ABYSS**. We fairies cannot travel there because of an **ancient enchantment** on the Infinite Abyss: Any fairy who tries to pass across the abyss will be **transformed** into an ordinary fish."

Pam shuddered. "**HOW SCARY!**"

The queen nodded. "Some of us, the bravest, have tried. But they have always come to a **sad** end."

Paulina got an excited look on her face. "It's a good thing we came here, then," she said. "We're not fairies. So we can **cross** the Infinite Abyss!"

I nodded. "That's **exactly** what we'll do. We'll find the Eel of Ages and find out who has stolen the Sea Violin."

"Thank you, strangers," said the queen. "But I must **warn** you. When you swim across the abyss, do not **look down** for any reason — or else the abyss will lure you into its **dark depths**," she added.

"I'm getting chills just thinking about it," said Violet.

"We will be careful," I promised.

"We have a **plan**," said Will. He turned to the queen. "Can you tell us how to reach the abyss?"

"I will give you a **MAP** of the realm," she answered. "But remember that the water currents can quickly change the path of the landscape."

"Thank you, Your Majesty," said Will. "The map will be very useful."

The queen took us to the **Hall of Royal Archives**. Hundreds of volumes of books told the **history** of the fairy realm.

"Here is your map," Anemone said, handing Will a rolled-up parchment. "Now my attendants will show you to your rooms, where you may rest before departing tomorrow."

As we left the hall, I heard Pam whisper to Colette.

"I hope there's **room service** in this castle," she said. "My stomach feels like an Infinite Abyss right now!"

Realm of Aquamarina

Colossus

Giant Sponge

Pink Pearl Castle

Turquoise Grotto

PLACID LAGOON

Coral Wall

INFINITE ABYSS

Evergreen Plain

Cave of the Eel of Ages

The Moving Dune and the
Cobalt Hermit Crab

Black Claw
Cove

Sirens' Bay and the
Emerald Sirens

WINDY CHANNEL

Sludge Pits and
Calamario

Cave of
Saledor

INTO THE ABYSS

The next morning, the queen's staff made us breakfast. We were refreshed and ready to go when the queen led us out of Pink Pearl Castle. We stopped at the coral wall.

"I will open the passageway for you, so that you may pass through unharmed," Queen Anemone said.

She waved her right hand, and the coral parted, leaving a **wide path** for us to go through.

"Go now," she told us. "I wish you success."

"THANK YOU, YOUR MAJESTY," Will replied. "We will do our best."

We swam away from the castle, making our way through the coral quickly this time.

Will looked at the **MAP** of Aquamarina as

we crossed the Placid Lagoon.

"We should keep going this way," he said. "It's the shortest route to the **INFINITE ABYSS**."

"I **hope** we can find the Sea Violin," Violet said as we swam.

"I hope so, too," said Colette. "This land is too beautiful to fade away forever."

Let's go!

This way!

"I'm curious about this Eel of Ages," said Pam. "A giant moray eel? Sounds like a **MONSTER**!"

"We've met all kinds of creatures in the fantasy worlds," I reminded her. "Sometimes the **SCARIEST-LOOKING** ones are the nicest and most helpful."

"I hope that's true," Pam said.

"Then maybe poor Queen Anemone won't look so **sad**," said Violet.

"We can try to save Aquamarina, but healing Anemone's **BROKEN HEART** might not be so easy," Nicky remarked.

A sudden *COLD CURRENT* shot up from the depths, making us shiver in spite of our wet suits. Below us we could see that we were coming to what looked like the edge of a cliff.

"I think we've arrived at the Infinite

Abyss!" Pam said.

Curious, she gazed over the edge. Then she suddenly TUMBLED forward!

Colette and I quickly grabbed her and pulled her back up.

"**WHoa!** The queen was right," said Pam. "There's a **POWERFUL FORCE** that pulls at anyone who looks down."

"We must be very careful," I said. "The slightest distraction could be very dangerous!"

"Let's all hold paws and form a chain as

Careful!

Ahhh!

we swim across," Will said.

"**Great idea, Will!**" said Paulina.

"Whatever you do, don't look down!" I warned.

"Don't worry," said Pam. "I won't make that **mistake** again. I don't want to find out what happens down there!"

We linked paws and then set off across the

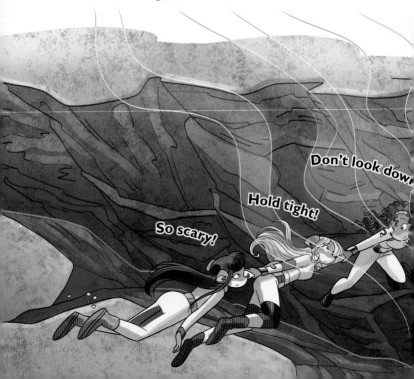

INFINITE ABYSS. We tried very hard to stare **straight ahead**, keeping our eyes on our goal: the cliffs on the other side. Would we make it without being swallowed into the **dark depths**?

"How's everyone doing?" I asked.

"I don't know, Thea," Nicky replied. "There's something **STRANGE** going on. I know that I shouldn't

This way!

Keep looking straight ahead!

look down, but it's as if a **COLD CURRENT** is trying to pull me to the bottom."

"That is the **challenge** of the abyss," said Will. "It's not going to be easy. But we can't give up!"

"Colette's right," said Violet, who was at the end of our chain. "I know I shouldn't look down, but I feel like I have to. **I can't resist!**"

"Violet, no!" Pam yelled.

Violet gazed into the abyss. Immediately, an **INVISIBLE FORCE** started to pull her down.

Colette didn't let go of Violet's paw.

"Vi, look at me! **YOU CAN DO IT!**" she yelled.

Pam held Colette's other paw. "Everyone, pull them up!"

We pulled with all our might, but the **FORCE** of the abyss was too **STRONG**. Colette's paw slipped out of Pam's and

Colette and Violet started to **SINK** down!

"**Noooooo!**" Pam cried.

Then I saw a *LIGHT* in Colette's eyes — a light of pure determination. She did not lose spirit. She gathered her **STRENGTH**, and **slowly** began to swim back up to us, pulling Violet with her.

I held my breath as Colette made her way *TOWARD* us,

finally grabbing hold of Pam's paw once more.

"**HOORAY!**" we all cheered.

"Colette, you saved me!" Violet said tearfully.

"Actually, it was our **friendship** that saved us," Colette told her. "When I looked in your eyes, I remembered how you've always been such a **good friend** to me. I didn't want to lose you. That gave me the **STRENGTH** to swim back up."

"**LET'S KEEP GOING!** We're almost there!" Will called out to us.

We **swam** over the edge of the abyss and onto a wide, underwater field. Green algae covered the ocean floor, **fluttering** in the current.

We had reached the Evergreen Plain.

DANGEROUS COILS

"We made it across the **INFINITE ABYSS**!" Nicky cheered.

"That was a **close call**," Pam said with a shudder.

Paulina gazed at the Evergreen Plain. "Luckily, we've entered a *peaceful* green field."

"Well, it *looks* peaceful," Will said, "but I've learned to be suspicious of places that are too quiet. Let's proceed with **CAUTION**."

We soon understood what Will meant. The algae leaves were so high and **BUSHY** that we couldn't see what dangers might be **Lurking** in them.

Will swam into the plain, and we followed him, keeping our eyes open. Suddenly, something red **DARTED** out of the algae!

"*It's a sea snake!*" Colette squeaked.

Nicky swam in front of her. She was from Australia and had encountered *snakes* many times before. She studied the bushy leaves.

"There's more than one, and they're very fast," she said.

"Careful, Nicky. They could be VENOMOUS," Will warned.

"True, but I've learned that it's best to **stay calm** around snakes," she said. "No sudden movements."

"So what should we do?" Pam asked.

"Let's **swim** higher," Nicky suggested.

"They might not be interested in us."

We started to swim higher when Pam cried out.

"My leg!"

A snake had wrapped itself around her leg! Another snake darted toward Colette, who **SCREAMED**.

"THEY'RE ATTACKING US!" I cried, dodging

Nooooo . . .

Let go!

Aaaaaaah!

a snake coming after me.

"Our wet suits will **PROTECT** us from any bites," Will said.

"But they're SQUEEZING us!" cried Pam.

"Keep swimming slowly away," said Nicky. "Maybe they'll give up."

But another snake *coiled* around Paulina's arm, and she gasped. Suddenly, I saw a light FLASH on her wet suit, and the snake hurried away from her.

Then I remembered that our wet suits all had built-in cameras.

"Paulina, is this the best time to be taking a PHOTOGRAPH?" Nicky asked her.

"I didn't do it on purpose," Paulina replied. "I must have turned it on by accident when the snake startled me."

I remembered how the snake had reacted to the flash.

"Paulina, take another picture!" I said.

Paulina looked puzzled, but she obeyed.

FLASH! Two snakes coming toward Paulina quickly swam away when they saw the light.

"They don't like the light!" Nicky realized. "Brilliant!"

"Everyone, use your cameras!" Will said.

FLASH! FLASH! FLASH!

The snakes didn't like the light at all. One by one, they swam away.

"HOORAY! They're leaving!" Violet cheered.

"Thank goodmouse," said Colette. "I'd give up my **whole wardrobe** if it meant I'd never have to see another snake again."

Everyone laughed, relieved to be out of danger once more.

"WAY TO GO, PAULINA!" I said.

"It was an accident," she said. "But I'm glad it worked!"

"We should *KEEP GOING*," Will said. "We're close to the eel's cave."

We swam forward, wondering what kind of welcome we would receive when we reached . . . the cave of the Eel of Ages!

BEYOND THE
EVERGREEN PLAIN

Will looked at the **MAP** as we swam across the Evergreen Plain.

"We should be seeing three **ROCKY PEAKS** soon," he said.

I looked around. All I could see in any direction was a carpet of green algae with long fronds.

"This plain seems *endless*," Nicky remarked.

I felt something **BRUSH** against my leg. Another snake? No, it was the algae!

"Look at the plants!" I cried. "They're **GROWING** in front of our eyes!"

"They're almost as TALL as we are!" Paulina exclaimed.

"Cheese niblets! My legs are getting all tangled up," said Pam.

"This plain looked beautiful from a distance, but it's really a NIGHTMARE," observed Violet.

Nicky nodded. "I thought after the snakes, our troubles would be over!"

"Just keep swimming," urged Will.

It keeps growing!

Let's keep going!

What now?

It's so tall!

Help!

"We'll get through this!"

We plodded through the algae as best as we could. But soon, the plants were so TALL and THICK that we couldn't see where we were and didn't know **which direction** to take.

Suddenly, Nicky cried out. "**LOOK!** A path!"

Sure enough, we saw a CLEAR PATH through the algae right in front of us.

"It seems to have come from nowhere," Paulina said.

"Will it lead us to the Eel of Ages?" Violet wondered.

"We'll only know if we follow it," said Nicky.

"But what if it's some kind of **TRICK**?" worried Colette.

"I'm afraid we'll have to take that chance,"

said Will. "The algae around us is TOO THICK to pass through."

We swam through the twisting path. Two high walls of algae rose up on either side of us.

"I think I can SEE something up ahead," Will said.

"I see it, too," I said. "It looks like rocks!"

The shape of the rocks became clearer as we swam closer.

"They're the THREE PEAKS!" Nicky cried.

"Thank goodmouse," said Colette.

"That must be the cave entrance there, by that **eerie red glow**," Pam said, pointing.

"Of course the Eel of Ages would live in a SPOOKY cave," said Colette. "I was kind of hoping for another **pearl palace**!"

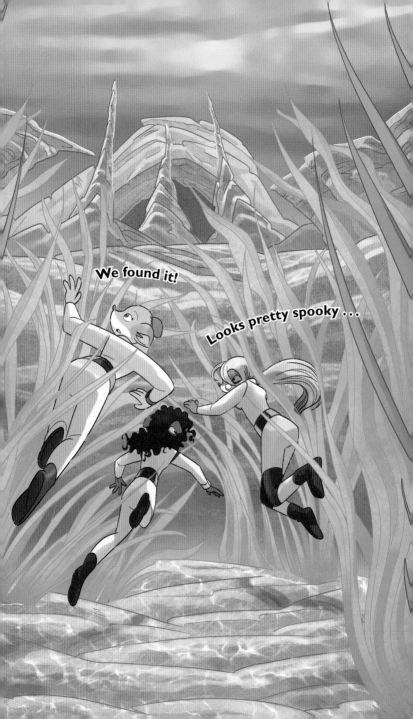

"I'll go first," Will said. "Turn on the **flashlights** in your wrist computers and follow me."

We all swam into the **DARK CAVE**.

"That's odd. I don't see a single plant or fish," Paulina remarked.

"That makes sense," said Nicky. "**Morays** eat fish. You'd have to be a pretty **BRAVE** fish to enter a moray's lair."

"Do morays eat mice, too?" Violet asked.

"Good question," said Nicky. "I don't really know."

A feeling of *uneasiness* came over us as we swam through the cave. It seemed to be endless.

But the **red glow** ahead was getting brighter as we went farther.

We swam toward the light and came upon a big purple moray eel **curled up** on a cushion. She stared at us **THREATENINGLY**.

We had found the Eel of Ages!

THE EEL'S TEST

The creature stared at us in *silence*. Next to her, on top of a pedestal, was the *Blue Pearl*. It looked almost like a crystal ball!

I stepped forward. "My name is Thea Stilton," I said. "My friends and I are here because we need your **HELP**."

The eel looked me right in the eye. "This is my cave, and I did not *invite* you here," she said in a deep, **CAVERNOUS** voice.

"I don't think she's happy to see us," Pam whispered to Colette.

Will stepped up next to me. "We **apologize** for invading your cave," he said. "But Aquamarina is in **TERRIBLE DANGER**. That is why we are here. We would like to consult the Blue Pearl."

The Eel of Ages burst into terrifying laughter. It echoed throughout the cave.

"How **DARE** you speak of the Blue Pearl?" she thundered.

"Queen Anemone advised us to seek it out," Will answered. "She said that it knows all of the secrets of the realm, and that only you can consult it."

What do you want?

We . . .

"And what do you wish to ask the pearl?" the eel inquired.

"The Sea Violin has been stolen," I replied. "Without the *Music of the Sea*, Aquamarina will slowly fade away. The marvelous **COLORS** of the sea creatures are already disappearing. We must find the **THIEF** and convince them to return the violin."

The eel nodded. "That is a NOBLE QUEST."

"Then you'll help us?" asked Colette.

"That is not up to me," replied the eel **mysteriously**.

"What do you mean?" asked Will.

"The Blue Pearl will aid only those who are **worthy** of it," answered the eel.

Will nodded. "I understand. How can we prove ourselves?"

"You must pass the test to demonstrate your **COURAGE** and the purity of your hearts," said the eel. "Only then will you be allowed to consult the Blue Pearl."

"What kind of test?" asked Pam.

"You will find out in time," said the eel. "But if you are not **BRAVE ENOUGH** to be tested, you can always return to Pink Pearl Castle."

"We are not afraid," said Will. "We will **PASS** the test, and then you will let us consult the Blue Pearl."

The Eel of Ages approached our friend and swirled three

Huh?

times around his body, moving very slowly. Then she wrapped her body around the pearl.

"THE PACT IS SEALED," she said.

"Please, Eel of Ages, tell us what the TEST is," I said.

"FOLLOW ME," she said, and she swam toward the entrance of the cave.

"Is this a TRICK after all?" Colette whispered. "It seems like she's leading us back outside the cave."

The eel spun around and stared at Colette. "I am no trickster! You will soon find out how serious I am."

Colette turned PALE, and we followed the eel in silence. She turned down a corridor and led us to a small room inside the cave. On the wall was a large oval MIRROR in a dark frame.

"That frame is made of **obsidian**," Will remarked.

Paulina nodded. "**VOLCANIC STONE**," she said, and the two exchanged a smile.

The Eel of Ages swam to the mirror.

"This is the **Mirror of Deep Truth**," she said. "The mirror will reveal your test, which comes in the form of three difficult **QUESTIONS** that you must seek the answers to. Are you ready?"

We all fell silent.

The eel began to draw circles on the mirror with her tail. The surface of the mirror **swirled**, and then words began to appear.

"It's the **FIRST QUESTION**!" Nicky exclaimed, swimming closer to the mirror. She read the words out loud.

WHAT COLOR ARE THE PETALS OF THE GOLDEN SUNLEAF?

"Petals . . . so the Golden Sunleaf must be some kind of flower," guessed Colette.

"But where can we find it?" asked Nicky.

"It only grows in the Forest of the Shallows," the eel answered. "It is west of here."

"How can there be a forest on the **seafloor**?" asked Paulina, but the eel didn't answer.

Instead, she **snickered** and then traced another circle on the mirror with her tail.

Once again, the mirror swirled, and a new question appeared:

HOW MANY PINK JELLYFISH ARE THERE IN AQUAMARINA?

"That's impossible," Colette said. "How can we **COUNT** every jellyfish in the ocean?"

"There is just one school of **pink jellyfish** in Aquamarina," answered the eel. "Finding them is part of your test."

"Finding them is just the beginning. Counting them won't be **EASY**, either," said Pam. "Jellyfish **STING**!"

"Fortunately, we have our **special wet suits** to protect us," Will reminded her.

The eel traced a circle on the mirror for a **THIRD** time.

WHAT TREASURE DO THE SEA NYMPHS OF SUNRISE QUARRY HOLD?

"Sea Nymphs sound much *friendlier* than jellyfish," Nicky remarked.

"They may not sting, but they guard their TREASURE closely," said the eel. "Finding the answer may not be as EASY as you think."

"How do we find them?" I asked.

"Again, finding them is part of your test," she replied. "I can only tell you that SUNRISE QUARRY is very ancient. The stone used to construct **Pink Pearl Castle** was taken from there."

Before we could ask any more questions, the Eel of Ages slipped away through a crevice in the rocky wall.

It was time to seek answers to our three questions — and save Aquamarina!

THE FOREST OF THE SHALLOWS

"We have **three** answers to find," said Violet. "What should we do first?"

"I think we should start with the **FIRST QUESTION**," said Colette. "At least we know that to get to the Forest of the Shallows, we have to travel west."

Nicky nodded. "That's right. We have no idea where the Sunrise Quarry is. Or how to find the **pink jellyfish**."

Will looked at his map. "There's nothing here about the quarry or the jellyfish. You're right, Colette. Let's head **west**."

"I'll check the **compass** on my computer," Paulina said, pressing a button on the sleeve of her wet suit. Then she

The compass will help us!

nodded. "It's that way."

We all started swimming west. After about twenty minutes we saw an enormouse expanse of **DARK GREEN** vegetation ahead of us.

"Do you think that could be the Forest of the Shallows?" asked Violet.

"It sure looks like a forest," said Pam.

When we got closer, we were amazed to be in an underwater jungle! **GREEN** algae bushes grew along the seafloor, and long **Vines** twisted around coral branches.

"Look over there!" Nicky hissed in a loud whisper. "Something's *moving*."

We turned to see a **PIXIE** with long green hair dart behind an algae bush. And she wasn't alone.

Several more pixies peeked out at us. They

wore dresses the same color as the plants and coral.

"Hello!" Pam said. "Do you know where we can find the **golden sunleaf**?"

But the frightened pixies scattered.

"I guess we should just try to look for flowers," suggested Nicky.

Then a school of winged fish swam by. Their heads were **brightly colored**, but their tails were Faded.

"I hope we find the flower soon," Violet said sadly. "The loss of the *Music of the Sea* is really starting to affect this world."

We swam through the forest, but we didn't find any flowers.

"I'm starting to **WORRY**," I whispered to Will, not wanting the others to hear.

He nodded. "This test is more difficult

than I thought it would be."

Just then, we saw the pixies again, flitting between branches of coral.

"Wait!" Nicky called out. "Can you please **HELP** us?" The pixies scattered again — except one, who hid behind what looked like a **red fruit**.

"Those look like tomatoes," Pam remarked.

The other **PIXIES** reappeared, swimming closer to Pam. They seemed less frightened now.

"I think we should check out those fruits," Pam said.

Look!

As we swam toward the fruit, we realized we were in a clearing. And it was filled with hundreds of the **bright red** fruits! Curiously, some of the green-haired fairies were **sleeping** on top of some of the fruits.

"The fruits look like jewels," said Colette.

"And they smell so sweet," Pam said, getting close to one.

At that moment, the fruit opened up to reveal a gorgeous flower with **ORANGE** petals.

"It's a **golden sunleaf**!" Violet cried.

"How can we be sure?" asked Pam. "It's a beautiful flower, but . . ."

"Try taking a few steps back, and follow the **LIGHT**," Violet suggested.

We all did as she said, and then we noticed it. A ray of sunlight had come through the water, landing on the flower.

"The **petals** open up when the sun hits them," said Colette.

"And then the PIXIES wake up," said

Paulina. "So that's why it's called the **golden sunleaf**!"

"That's right," I said. "And we also have the answer to our first question. The petals of the Golden Sunleaf are **orange**!"

"One **question** down, two to go," said Pam.

Do you see?

THE DANCE OF THE PINK JELLYFISH

"We still don't know **which way** to go," Nicky pointed out.

"Let's head **OUT** of the Forest of the Shallows and then check the map," Will suggested.

We agreed, and wove through *tangled vines* until we found ourselves on the edge of a cliff. Then we swam across the **ABYSS** that had opened up below us. Luckily, this time there was no *mysterious* force pulling us downward: just many **FISH** of every shape and color.

"Amazing! I've never seen so many fish at once!" exclaimed Violet.

"Me neither, Vi! They're as colorful as flowers," Colette observed with delight.

Then Violet frowned. "Yes, but some of their colors are Fading."

"We've got to get the Sea Violin back into Queen Anemone's hands," said Nicky.

"I hope we can figure out where to go next," said Pam.

"Any LUCK with the map, Will?" I asked.

Will shook his head. "Not yet."

Then Violet swam toward a large, purple-

Careful!

So cute...

and-yellow fish.

"Look how big and ROUND this fish is," she remarked.

"It's a **BLOWFISH**!" warned Nicky. "Be careful. They're SHARP!"

"Sharp? But it's so cute, like a balloon," said Violet.

"It BLOWS UP when it feels threatened," Nicky told her. "A blowfish swallows water to make it look BIGGER and frighten predators. It's also covered in pointed spines so that other fish won't eat it!"

"It's a good thing you know so much about fish, Nicky," Colette said. "Are there any others we should worry about?"

"It's hard to tell," Nicky replied. "Who knows what STRANGE CREATURES we might find here in Aquamarina!"

"I'm sure we'll find many," Will said. "Let's keep swimming."

As we swam, the water became shallower. Below us we could see **tunnels**, caves, and curious rock structures that stretched out like a MAZE.

"What's that up ahead?" Violet asked. "Those creatures look like pink **butterflies**."

I followed Violet's gaze. Pink creatures fluttered through the water.

"They're the **pink jellyfish**!" I said. "Now we can answer our second question."

"But how do we **count** them? There are so many," Paulina said.

"And I don't think we should get any closer," added Pam. "Those tentacles

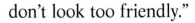

don't look too friendly."

"I know that they're dangerous, but they look so **elegant**," Colette remarked. "They remind me of **dancers** in fluffy organza gowns."

Paulina lit up. "Colette, can you repeat what you just said?"

"Um, the jellyfish look like they're wearing **gowns**?" Colette repeated, uncertainly.

"Not that part — you said they looked like **dancers**!" Paulina exclaimed. "That gave me an idea, although I'm not sure if it will work."

Will smiled. "Give it a try. You always have great ideas!"

Paulina smiled back. "Thanks. Here's what I'm thinking. Do you see how the jellyfish move? They **WAVE** along with the current."

"Almost like they're dancing!" said Violet.

"**EXACTLY!**" Paulina said. "What if we manage to draw them into a kind of a dance? It we could get them all to *FOLLOW ALONG* and line up, they'll be easier to count."

Will nodded **thoughtfully**. "That might work."

I quickly turned Paulina's idea into a plan. "Okay, Colette, Violet, and Paulina will start dancing and get the jellyfish to follow them. Nicky and Pam will get on the end of the line. And Will and I will **count them** as they swim by that **POINTY** rock over there."

We all got into position, and Colette started to swim as if she were dancing.

Paulina and Violet imitated her, flapping

their arms like butterfly wings.

A moment later, one of the jellyfish danced toward them, waving its tentacles. A second jellyfish followed behind it, and then a third, and a fourth . . .

What a SPECTACLE of grace and harmony! The dance of the pink jellyfish was so beautiful that it took our breath away.

But Will and I had to concentrate on our task, and we carefully counted each jellyfish as it passed by.

"One hundred and three jellyfish!" I cried when the last creature had danced past us.

Paulina recorded the number on her computer.

"Great job, Paulina," Will said. "Your plan worked! Now we just have to figure out how to find Sunrise Quarry . . ."

THE MOODY
MOLLUSKS

"Maybe we can find a pixie or another creature who can give us **directions**," Nicky suggested.

So we swam forward, hoping to find someone who could help us. We swam and swam with no luck.

"**Cheese and crackers!**" Pam moaned. "We're so close to passing our test, but I feel like we'll never do it!"

"We must have FAITH," I told her. "In fact, I think I see something moving up ahead!"

As we swam closer, we saw two **strange-looking mollusks** ahead of us. Each had a shell on its head and long **arms** sticking out.

"It looks like they're **BUILDING** something," Nicky remarked.

They appeared to be making a hut out of **PINK** and **BLUE** stones, and they looked very busy. As soon as they saw us, they stared at us suspiciously.

"**Who are you, and what do you want?**" asked the mollusk with a green shell.

"We are sorry to disturb you —" I began, but he interrupted me.

"That's right! You're **disturbing** us! So please get out of here!" he said, waving me away with his arms.

"We just need some information," I pressed on. "It won't take long."

"We don't have any time to help you," the mollusk said. "My wife and I must finish building our house before the **CURRENT** arrives."

"What current?" I asked.

His wife rolled her eyes. "You DON'T KNOW anything, do you?"

"And anyway, we don't have time to talk to you now!" her husband added.

"There's no reason to be **RUDE**," Colette told them.

The mollusk looked at her, rolled his large, **ROUND EYES**, and put down one of the rocks he was moving.

"Why oh why can't I get any **peace** today?" he wailed. "Earlier, a **HERMIT CRAB** came and destroyed our home — he took all of our seashells!"

Leave us alone!

"I'm so **sorry** to hear that," Colette said sympathetically.

"So that's why you are so *busy* building your home."

"Right! And we don't have time to waste chit-chatting!" he snapped.

"We understand, but could you **please** answer our question?" Colette asked.

"Will you **GO** if I do?" he asked suspiciously.

"I promise," I replied.

Just one question

What do you want?

"Okay then," he said with a **sigh**. "What do you want to know?"

"Where did you get those **BEAUTIFUL** stones you are using to build your house?" I asked.

"**HA!** I get it now!" the mollusk cried. "You want to **TAKE AWAY** our stones. Well, you can't have them!"

"We don't want your stones," I said. "But we are trying to find **Sunrise Quarry**."

"Did you get your stones from there?" asked Paulina. "And if you did, can you **kindly** tell us how to get there?"

The mollusk **GLARED** at us.

"Why do you want to go to Sunrise Quarry?" he asked.

"We are searching for the **Sea Nymphs**, to learn about their treasure," Colette told him.

"**Impossible**," he said, shaking his head.

"Their treasure is a great secret!"

"We know, but we have to **TRY** to find it," Colette said.

"Why are you so interested in it?" asked the mollusk's wife.

"It's a long story, but the **safety** of Aquamarina depends on it," Will chimed in.

"That includes you and your new house," Colette pointed out.

"This house is already an **ABYSS'S WORTH** of work!" the mollusk cried. Then he frowned, thinking. "If I help you, what do I get for it?"

Colette thought quickly. "How about a *fuchsia hair tie*?"

"What's a hair tie?" the mollusk asked.

Colette removed the hair tie from her blonde hair. "It's **stretchy**," she told him. "You could tie clumps of algae together with it, or attach two rocks together, or use it as a decoration."

The mollusk was intrigued. "All right, you have a deal!"

Colette gave him the hair tie, and the mollusk POINTED with one of his arms.

"Go **that way**, to the end of the boulders," he instructed. "Then wait for the CURRENT. It will be here soon, and it will take you right to the quarry."

The current will carry you . . .

Thanks!

"Are you sure?" asked Nicky.

"Do I look like a liar to you?" the mollusk snapped.

"Of course not! Sorry," said Nicky.

"Thanks for your help," I said quickly.

"You're welcome," said the mollusk. "Now scram!"

"And good luck!" his wife added, smiling.

"Good luck building your house," Violet called behind her as we swam away.

We could hear the mollusk CALLING after us as we left.

"Nothing is as it seems!" he yelled. "Remember that when you meet the nymphs!"

"What an odd mollusk," Paulina remarked.

"And cranky, too," Pam said.

Then, just as the mollusk had said, the CURRENT came and carried us far away.

THE SEA NYMPHS

Soon the OCEAN CURRENT stopped pushing us and left us in calm water on a plateau of dark rock. It was embedded with pieces of milky **mother-of-pearl**.

"Mother-of-pearl is so **pretty**," Violet remarked, stroking the stone with her paw. "It's the lining of seashells, isn't it?"

"That's right!" Nicky said.

"The Sunrise Quarry must be somewhere nearby," said Will, looking around.

"We've got to be **CLOSE**," Nicky agreed, swimming forward. "Come on!"

We followed her to the **EDGE** of the plateau — and our jaws dropped!

The inside of the mountain had been excavated, and a **VILLAGE** had been constructed in the open space. *Green plants* grew over the stone houses.

"**INCREDIBLE!**" Nicky exclaimed.

"This must be where the Sea Nymphs live," I observed.

"I hope they're **NICER** than those mollusks," Colette said.

"Yes, nice enough to tell us where they're

hiding their treasure," Pam added.

"Let's find out!" Nicky said, swimming down into the village.

"Slow down," Will warned. "We should STICK TOGETHER until we know how these nymphs feel about visitors."

As we swam toward the village, Violet sniffed the air. "Do you smell that?"

"Yes. Something smells DELICIOUS!" agreed Colette.

Pam's stomach growled. "It's reminding me how **hungry** I am!"

We touched down on the floor of the quarry. A nymph came out of the house in front of us. She wore a pretty **PINK** tunic and carried what looked like a **PIE**.

The nymph stopped when she saw us, and we smiled at her.

"Hello," Will said.

The nymph remained silent. A second nymph carrying a tray of cookies joined her, and they exchanged a look of SURPRISE.

More nymphs came forward, surrounding us. They stared at us without saying a word.

"Please pardon the *INTRUSION*," I said. "We don't want to disturb you."

"It looks like we've **interrupted** your

meal," said Colette, with a nod to the plates they were carrying.

The nymphs continued to **STARE** at us, and we started to feel uncomfortable.

"Maybe they don't *understand* what we're saying," Nicky suggested.

"Or maybe they don't COMMUNICATE with words," Paulina guessed.

Finally, the nymph

Excuse us . . . Are we disturbing you?

holding the **PIE** took a step toward us.

"Welcome to the Sunrise Quarry, kind guests," she said. Her voice was as **sweet** and MELODIOUS as a flute. "I am Maira."

"And I am Halia," said the nymph holding the cookies. "Please *forgive us* for not speaking up right away. We did not mean to be **impolite**."

We all let out a *sigh* of relief.

"You don't need to apologize," Will said. "We are sorry to come without an invitation, but we are here for a **very important** reason."

"What reason?" Maira asked.

"We are trying to save **Aquamarina**,

and you can help us," Will replied.

"Us? How?" asked Halia.

"We're seeking answers to three questions," answered Paulina. "We need to find out what precious treasure you guard."

Halia shook her head. "We can't tell you that."

"Why not?" asked Violet, surprised.

"It is not for us to reveal," said Maira. "Our treasure only reveals itself to those who are WORTHY."

We looked at one another sorrowfully. What were we going to do now?

"You must be hungry," Maira said. "Please, sit down at our table with us."

"We will speak more as we eat," added Halia with a

mysterious smile.

"We GLADLY accept your invitation," Will said.

The Sea Nymphs led us to a **taBLe** topped with food. More nymphs joined us.

"Wow, this all looks **delicious**!" exclaimed Pam.

"Try this algae pie," offered Maira.

"And I baked some CooKies," said Halia.

We all sat down and began to eat.

THE LOOM OF HAPPINESS

The Sea Nymphs were very **kind** and **hospitable** to us. I hoped once we knew them better, they might **reveal** their secret to us.

"Now Galene and I have something to **show** you," said Maira, nodding to another nymph when our meal was done.

The two nymphs led us into one of the stone houses. It was **simple**, but welcoming. In the middle of the room was a large **loom** made of golden wood. Someone had started weaving a piece of cloth on it.

Galene handed Colette a *golden spool*.

"This is **MISSING** its thread," Colette remarked.

The nymph smiled. "You don't **SEE** the thread, but it's there."

"I don't understand," said Colette.

"You will understand if you weave," Galene promised.

Colette sat down and started to pass the spool from one side of the loom to the other. Or at least, she tried.

"It's not working!" she said.

"Free your **MIND** and your **heart**," Maira coached her.

Colette tried again, but soon she shook her head. "I can't do it."

"Can I try?" Nicky asked.

Nicky took the spool and passed it through the threads on the loom, but once again, NOTHING happened.

"I don't see the thread, and I don't **feel** it, either," she said, frustrated.

The nymphs watched carefully as Violet tried next, and then Paulina, with no luck.

"My turn!" said Pam.

Pam took the spool, closed her eyes, and tried to think about something that made her **happy**. To our great surprise, we could see thread appear as Pam passed the spool BACK and FORTH across the loom. Little by little, the weaving **TOOK SHAPE** before our eyes.

"Pam! You're doing it!" cried Violet.

Pam opened her eyes.

"Did I really do that?" she asked in wonder.

"Yes!" I replied.

Pam looked carefully

My turn!

at the images woven on the cloth. "It's us!"

"On the night of your **birthday**," Paulina remembered.

"When we all made you that great **PIZZA**," added Nicky.

Pam nodded. "That was the best birthday present ever!"

"We were happy to give it to you!" said Colette. "We're your friends!"

The two nymphs smiled at each other, nodding.

"You have discovered the secret of the *Loom of Happiness*," said Galene. "It was given to us by Queen Anemone's grandmother as a symbol of her gratitude, because the stones that build Pink Pearl Castle were mined from Sunrise Quarry."

"So it's true that the castle stones came from here!" said Will.

"Yes, and they are very special stones, because they are able to contain good feelings," said Galene.

"Just like the loom's fabric," added Maira.

"What do you mean?" asked Colette.

"When woven together, the threads tell the story of our feelings," explained Maira. "Events and people who stir our emotions become visible in the fabric when we free our hearts. And there's just one thing that makes this all possible."

"What is it?" asked Will.

"This," the two nymphs replied. They slowly pressed their palms together. When they pulled them apart, a thin thread made of pure light stretched between them.

"This thread represents the tie of **friendship** between us," said Galene.

"So, Pam was able to **WEAVE** the cloth because she was thinking about friendship?" asked Violet.

Here . . .

Look!

"That's right," said Maira. "By thinking of the AFFECTION that connects you, she made the thread appear."

Pam nodded. "That's true. Although the first thing I thought about was the tasty cheese pizza."

We all laughed.

"But then I thought about all of the nice things you've done for me, and how close we've been," Pam concluded, looking at the Thea Sisters.

"Group hug!" shouted Nicky, and they all hugged one another tightly.

"Friends forever!" the mouselets sang out.

The nymphs, Will, and I looked on with tears in our eyes.

"Now can you show us the treasure?" Will asked the nymphs. "We need to know what it is in order to consult the *Blue Pearl*."

"We need to find out who stole the queen's **Sea Violin**," I added. "Without its music, your world will **disappear**."

The nymphs were silent.

Then I looked at the **THEA SISTERS** and realized that the answer was right in front of my eyes!

"I get it!" I cried. "We've already found the treasure!"

The nymphs nodded and smiled. "Yes. **FRIENDSHIP** is the greatest treasure that exists."

"We've done it! We've answered the **third question**!" Will cheered.

It was the end of a **long day**. We stayed in the village of the Sea Nymphs and got a good night's sleep.

THE BLUE PEARL

The next morning we woke up rested and ready to get back to the Eel of Ages. We were anxious to pass her test with answers to all three questions. So we said good-bye to our new nymph friends and swam back to the eel's cave.

When we got there, we found the eel curled up on her cushion.

"You've returned at last," she said. "Can you answer the three questions?"

"We can," Will replied.

"Good. Then APPROACH," she ordered.

We obeyed, and she asked us the first question.

"Tell me: **What color are the petals of the Golden Sunleaf?**" she asked.

"**ORANGE**," Pam replied.

The moray smiled. "Correct. Now, to the second question: **How many pink jellyfish are there?**"

Paulina checked the number on her wrist computer. "One hundred and three," she said confidently.

The eel's eyes widened. "Are you sure?"

"Of course. We **counted** them," Paulina replied.

An irritated look crossed the eel's face. No one had ever gotten this far before. "Correct. Now to the final question: **What is the treasure of the Sea Nymphs of the Sunrise Quarry?**"

The Thea Sisters looked at Will and me, and we understood. They wanted to answer this one together.

"**FRIENDSHIP**," they said. "The Sea

Nymphs' treasure is friendship."

As soon as they spoke, the Blue Pearl flashed with silver light.

"What's happening?" asked Will.

"The *Blue Pearl* has deemed you worthy," the Eel of Ages said. "It is ready to answer your question."

"May we ask it now?" I asked.

"**watch and wait**," answered the eel. Then the Eel of Ages swam around and around the Blue Pearl. The pearl began to SHINE like a star in the night sky.

"We'd like to ask it who stole the Sea Violin," Will said.

"I know," said the eel, continuing to wind

around the pearl. "And so does the pearl. See for yourself."

We all stared at the Blue Pearl.

Suddenly, the LIGHT inside the sphere went out. Then it quickly lit up again. Colorful lights flashed from the pearl, projecting a series of IMAGES on the wall of the cave, one after another. They appeared so quickly that it was difficult to tell what we were seeing. An underwater MOUNTAIN? A large FISH?

The Eel of Ages kept circling the Blue Pearl. When she finally stopped, the light Faded from the pearl, but it was still a SPLENDID JEWEL.

The eel settled back onto her cushion. "The pearl has given you its response," she announced. "It is true that someone has stolen the Sea Violin."

"Who was it?" Colette asked **eagerly**.

"The pearl did not say," the eel replied.

A wave of disappointment crashed over us.

"Then how will we find it?" Pam wondered.

"The pearl did not give a name, but it showed a **location** where you will find whoever stole the violin," the eel replied.

We were hopeful once more. "**Where is it?**" I asked.

"You will find the thief at the **MOVING DUNE**, a desert zone in the northern part of the realm," answered the eel.

Will nodded. "I remember seeing it on the **MAP**," he said, unrolling the parchment that the queen had given him. He pointed to a spot. "It's right here."

"We must go there **right away**," I said.

"I warn you, it will be a **DIFFICULT** journey,

full of **danger**," said the Eel of Ages. "And there's one more thing you must know before you depart."

"What's that?" Colette asked.

"Keep a close **EYE** on the thief," she replied. "There is a veil of mystery around the one who stole the violin."

"What kind of mystery?" asked Will.

"I have nothing more to say. This is all the *pearl* has revealed," the eel said.

"I guess we'll **FIND OUT** when we find the thief!" said Pam.

"Thank you, Eel of Ages," Will said. "We have to go now."

She nodded. "Good luck in your task."

As we left the **CAVE** I glanced back. The eel was watching us with a gaze that seemed *sad*, as if she was sorry to see us go.

HEEEEEEELP!

"The Eel of Ages was very kind in the end," Colette said as we swam away from the cave.

"Yes," agreed Paulina. "She seemed a little sorry that we were leaving."

"It must be very **lonely** in that cave," Violet said sympathetically.

"I just can't believe the Blue Pearl didn't give us the **name** of the thief," said Pam. "How will we know who to look for when we get to the Moving Dune?"

"We'll figure it out," Will said confidently. He stopped and unrolled the map again. "First, we need to determine where we're going."

Paulina looked over his shoulder. "It looks

The Windy Channel! Hmm . . .

like we need to cross the Windy Channel," she said.

"That name doesn't sound too promising," Nicky remarked.

"And first we'll have to cross back over the Infinite Abyss!" said Pam.

"We can face any **difficulty** if we do it together," I reassured them.

We started swimming toward the Windy Channel.

"We've got a *long trip* ahead of us," said Will. "Let's swim slowly to save our energy."

So we moved ahead at a **STEADY PACE**. As we swam, we could see more and more fish with faded colors.

"**Those poor fish!**" cried Violet.

"This world really is slowly disappearing," said Colette.

"We can't let it happen. We won't!" Pam cried.

"That's the spirit!" Will cheered.

We were more determined than ever to save Aquamarina. But before long we felt a **light current** pushing against us.

"This current is slowing us down!" Nicky remarked.

The current quickly got **STRONGER** — so strong that it was almost impossible to swim against.

"**I can't go forward!**" Violet cried.

"Me neither!" said Pam.

We were all **struggling**. I looked around for something we could grab on to — a rock or an algae bush — but there was nothing around us except for **water**. In seconds, the current would push us away from our goal.

"**LOOK THERE!**" Pam cried suddenly, pointing.

A **POD OF DOLPHINS** was swiftly swimming toward us.

"We've got to get out of their way," said Paulina. "They might swim into us!"

"**I CAN'T MOVE**," wailed Violet.

This current . . .

Oof!

Help!

. . . is so strong!

Be brave!

"This current is too strong!"

None of us could fight the **POWERFUL FORCE** of the current.

"The dolphins are getting closer!" Pam warned.

What could we do?

"These **DOLPHINS** might be just what we need!" Nicky cried. "They're *friendly* animals. Maybe they'll give us a ride!"

"Let's give it a try!" I urged.

It worked!

When the dolphins swam by, we asked them for help. The friendly animals were happy to give us rides! We climbed onto their backs and took off.

THE FIERCE BLACK CLAW CREW

"Thank you, dolphin friends," I said after we had JOURNEYED across the Windy Channel.

"Happy to help!" said the dolphin who had given me a ride.

"*You are so kind,*" said Violet, giving a gentle pat to the dolphin who had carried her.

"You never would have managed it alone," said the dolphin. "The Windy Channel has the strongest and most **DANGEROUS** current in the whole realm."

"We noticed that!" I said.

"We have one more **favor** to ask, if you don't mind," said Will. "Could you please tell us how to find the Moving Dune?"

You have been so kind . . .

The dolphins shared a worried look. Then one of them flicked his tail to the left.

"It's that way," he said. "But to reach it, you have to cross **BLACK CLAW COVE**."

"Is it dangerous?" I asked.

"It can be," replied the dolphin. "It's the territory of the **BLACK CLAW CREW**. They're known for **robbing** travelers."

"What's the Black Claw Crew?" asked Colette.

"They're fierce **PiRATES**," the dolphin said. "You must be careful!"

"And there's no other way to reach the MOVING DUNE?" Will asked.

The dolphin shook his head. "I'm afraid not."

We said good-bye to the dolphins and swam toward the Moving Dune. The water became shallower, and the sand stretched out in front of us like an underwater desert.

"Let's proceed carefully," said Will. "The pirates could be anywhere."

"We can get a better view from that DUNE," Nicky said, nodding toward a hill of sand up ahead.

We swam to it and **PEERED** over the edge.

"Look! I see houses," said Pam.

Violet gasped. "And there's a **PIRATE SHIP**!"

The ship had **black** sails and a giant crustacean tail and claws. Three **BIG FISH** were tied to the ship with seaweed vines.

"This must be **BLACK CLAW COVE**!" Colette realized.

"It has to be," said Paulina. "Look at the side of the ship. It says **CLAW OF THE DEEP**."

"Do you think the **THIEF** we're looking for is one of the pirates?" asked Nicky. "The dolphin told us they were **robbers**."

"It's possible," I said. "That means the Sea Violin could be hidden around here somewhere."

"Let's look for it!" cried Pam, eager to take action.

"This could be **DANGEROUS**," said Will.

"Thea and I will go first. If it looks safe, we'll signal you."

"Can't I come with you?" Pam asked.

"It's better if the five of you stay here," I said, agreeing with Will.

The mouselets looked disappointed.

"Don't worry," I reassured them. "You'll get a chance to explore."

So Will and I swam down into Black Claw Cove while the mouselets hid and waited. It was EERILY quiet.

We had no idea if danger awaited us — but we knew we couldn't back down now!

SURPRISE ATTACK!

"Let's head for the ship," I whispered as we swam into the cove. "Maybe the Sea Violin is hidden there."

Will nodded and we swam toward the **CLAW OF THE DEEP**. Suddenly, I felt someone tap on my shoulder.

Startled, I turned to see a **LOBSteR** wearing a pirate's black bandanna!

"**INTRUDERS!**" yelled the lobster. "**CAPTURE THEM, CREW!**"

A **CRAB** wearing an eye patch quickly appeared, followed by a PRAWN wearing a bandanna.

Intruders!

"**SHIVER ME SEASHELLS!**" cried the crab. "I'll bet you a **barrel of algae** that they're here to steal our gold."

"Well, I'll bet you **TWO BARRELS**!" said the lobster.

"**THREE BARRELS!**" cried the prawn.

A woman's voice broke through the arguing.

"What's going on here?"

Huh?

Uh?

Captain Aragosa

The crustaceans stood at attention. "**CAPTAIN ARAGOSA!**"

"Who are these intruders?" asked the woman. She had long black hair. She carried a **SWORD** and wore a pirate's hat. "Have you questioned them?"

"I was about to when Crabby challenged me," said the lobster.

The pirate captain sighed. "Do I have to do

What's going on?

everything myself?" she asked.

"**Yes, Captain!**" the pirates shouted.

Aragosa shook her head and turned to us. "I'm sure you two have a **good reason** for coming here. Don't they, crew?"

"**Yes, Captain!**" the pirates cried.

Will smiled at her. "We are very sorry to disturb you, Captain," he said.

Aragosa raised an eyebrow. "You can try to sweet talk me, but it won't save you."

"**Aye, Captain!**" exclaimed the pirates.

She glared at them. "Shut your traps and seize them!"

The lobster wrapped his claws around Will, and the prawn grabbed me.

Aragosa smiled at us. "I am **CAPTAIN ARAGOSA**, leader of the Black Claw Crew. We do not allow intruders in our territory. You both are now our **prisoners!**"

The pirates couldn't help themselves.

"**HOORAY FOR ARAGOSA!**" they cheered.

Will and I exchanged worried glances. Being CAPTURED BY PIRATES wasn't part of our plan!

"Please, Captain," I said. "Before you take us prisoner, you should at least find out who we are and why we are here."

We're here for a reason . . .

What's that?

Aragosa **SNEERED** at me. "If it's so important to you, stranger, then **speak!**"

"My name is Thea Stilton, and this is Will Mystery," I began. "We've come from very **far away**, because we learned that Aquamarina is in danger. We need to find the Sea Violin so we can save your land!"

To our surprise, Aragosa burst out laughing. "And you came to find the Sea Violin here? What would we want with such a worthless object?"

"It is far from worthless," said Will. "Queen Anemone must play it every night to produce the magic that keeps your world alive."

"Queen Anemone, eh?" said the pirate captain thoughtfully. "If we find it ourselves, we can demand a **HANDSOME RANSOM** from her!"

"**Great idea, Captain!**" said the pirates.

"We'll take on the royal guard if we must," said Aragosa.

"**Brilliant, Captain!**" the pirates cheered.

"Stop your compliments and let me think," said Aragosa. "Lock up these two landlubbers while I figure out our next move."

"Aye, Captain!"

The pirates pushed us through a long tunnel in the sand. Below the ground was a **labyrinth** of rooms and hallways!

They led us to a cell with a **rusty** iron door.

"I think they'll be **comfortable** here, Shelly," Crabby said to the prawn.

"That's right," Shelly said, glaring at us. "And don't you two try to **ESCAPE**. It's impossible!"

Then they **PUSHED** us into the cell and closed the **HEAVY** door behind us.

Will and I frowned at each other.

"Well, this is a pickle we're in," Will said.

I nodded. "Definitely. We need to find a way to **GET OUT**!"

The thick iron door looked **IMPOSSIBLE** to break through. But we had to try!

LET'S DO SOMETHING!

Meanwhile, the THEA SISTERS were starting to worry about me and Will.

"It's been a half hour, and they aren't back yet," Pam said.

"Do you think they're in **trouble**?" asked Violet.

"**I DO**," said Colette. "We need to do something!"

"We should swim to the **PiRATES'** cove and look for them," Nicky suggested.

"That's a good idea, but we need a PLAN," Paulina said. "They might have been **captured**. We don't want to end up in the pirates' clutches, too."

"You're right," Violet agreed.

"So what's our plan, then?" asked Nicky.

Colette looked **thoughtful**. "Maybe we could get the pirates to leave the cove first."

"How could we do that?" asked Pam.

"There must be a way to get them to board their ship and **sail away** from here," Colette replied. "We just need to **think**."

Suddenly, Nicky cried out. "Look over there! It's the dolphins!"

Thank you!

The same pod of **DOLPHINS** that we'd met before was swimming toward them.

"Maybe they'll **HELP** us again," Violet said.

Colette nodded. "I think I have a plan."

She swam to the dolphins

and explained her idea.

"Sure, we'd be **happy** to help you," one of the dolphins replied.

"That's why we returned — to make sure you were okay," another said.

Colette hugged him. "Thank you so much!"

The two dolphins swam into the middle of the cove and spoke **LOUDLY** enough for any hidden pirates to hear.

"It **SANK** with all its cargo? Are you sure?" the first dolphin asked.

"Yes, Long Fin saw it with his own eyes," said the second dolphin. "The ship wrecked not far from the Windy Channel."

"What was the ship carrying? Jewels?" asked the first.

"Jewels and gold," replied the second. "A ton of TREASURE."

Then they swam away. Crabby and Shelly PEEKED out of a hole in the sand.

"Did you hear that, Crabby?" asked Shelly.

"I sure did, Shelly," Crabby replied.

"We've got to tell ARAGOSA right away!" said Shelly. "I'm already DROOLING at the thought of all that gold."

"QUICK! Let's go find her!" Crabby said. They hurried off to tell their captain about the treasure.

Back at the dune, the dolphins filled in the THEA SISTERS.

"I'm sure they heard us," said the first dolphin.

"I saw the sand move right near us," said

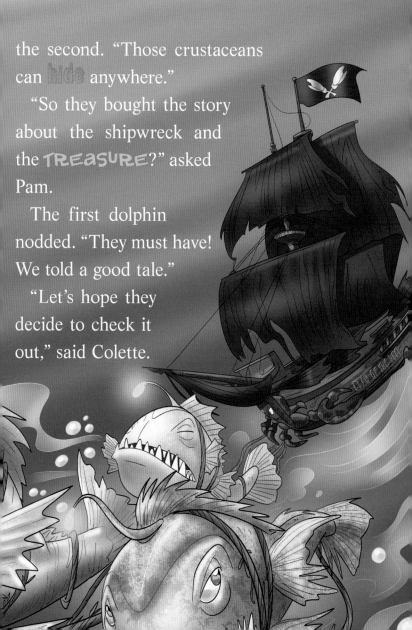

the second. "Those crustaceans can hide anywhere."

"So they bought the story about the shipwreck and the TREASURE?" asked Pam.

The first dolphin nodded. "They must have! We told a good tale."

"Let's hope they decide to check it out," said Colette.

"No **PIRATE** can resist treasure!" the second dolphin assured her.

Soon the crustacean pirates appeared, scurrying onto the **CLAW OF THE DEEP**. Then Captain Aragosa walked onto the ship.

"**Who's that?**" asked Violet. (The Thea Sisters were seeing her for the first time.)

"Captain Aragosa, leader of the Black Claw Crew," answered the dolphin. "She is a **clever** and **FEARSOME** pirate."

Where are Will and Thea?

Hmm . . .

So quiet!

Aragosa might be clever, but she fell for Colette's trick. The pirate ship sailed away from the cove in search of the shipwreck!

"Thank you, dolphin friends!" said Violet.

"We'd do anything to save our world," one of them replied.

"Now let's go find Will and Thea!" urged Colette.

The pirates are gone!

Here's a tunnel . . .

The Thea Sisters quickly swam into the cove.

"Could they have locked up Will and Thea in a **PRISON** somewhere?" Nicky wondered.

Then Paulina spotted a tunnel in the sand. "Maybe they're down here!"

The Thea Sisters dove into the tunnel and swam through the undersea labyrinth. They quickly reached the hallway full of **IRON DOORS**.

"These look like prison cells," Colette remarked.

"**Will! Thea!**" they all called out.

Will and I were so happy to hear their voices.

"**WE'RE HERE! WE'RE LOCKED INSIDE!**" we shouted in reply.

A PRISONER MADE OF GOLD

"Thea? Will? Let us know **WHICH DOOR** you're behind!" Paulina shouted.

"**WE'RE HERE!**" I yelled, pounding on the door.

Seconds later, Paulina's face peered through the bars.

"We found you!" she cried happily.

"Are you okay? Did they hurt you?" Violet asked.

"No, they just **LOCKED** us in here," Will replied.

We're here!

"Is there a **Key** out there?" I asked.

"We'll find it," Pam said confidently.

The Thea Sisters swam up and down the row of cells.

"I don't **SEE** a key," Paulina reported.

"Me neither!" the others chimed in.

Colette pulled a **PIN** out of her hair. "Maybe this will work," she said. She stuck it into the lock and *jiggled* it. Then she frowned. "No luck."

"I hope the **PIRATES** didn't take it with them," Violet fretted.

"They're gone?" I asked.

"Yes, thanks to a little *trick*," Colette replied. "We can explain later — but we need to get you out of here."

"Where is that **Key**?" Pam wondered.

Suddenly, an unfamiliar voice spoke up.

"The key that opens all the cells is hidden

in the keyhole of the first door on the left."

"**Who said that?**" Colette asked.

"I did," replied the voice. "Third cell on the right."

The mouselets went to the cell and **LOOKED** through the bars. A glimmering fish swam up to them.

"Who are you?" asked Paulina.

"I am the Golden Fish," he replied.

"Are you made of gold?" Pam asked.

"Yes, my scales are," the fish replied.

"Amazing!" cried Colette. "Is that why the **PIRATES** have locked you in this cell?"

I'm the Golden Fish!

"Yes, they wanted to take my golden scales," the fish replied. "But they realized that as soon as you touch them, they become just like any other fish scales."

"*Good thing!*" Pam cried.

"So why didn't they let you go?" Nicky asked.

"They were **convinced** they could find a way to take my scales without them changing," the fish answered.

"We'll get you out of here!" Paulina promised.

She rushed to get the key, right where the fish had said it was. Then she **FREED** us all.

"Thank you, agents! You have done GREAT WORK, as always," Will praised them.

I hugged them. "Thank you! I didn't enjoy being locked up."

"I'm so glad we found you and got you out of there," Paulina said tearfully.

I turned to the Golden Fish. "*Thank you* for helping us, too."

"It is I who must thank you," the fish said. "If you hadn't arrived, I might have been in that **cell** for a long time."

"We were **happy** to help you," said Colette.

"Um, this is a nice reunion, but those

Thanks, friends!

We're free!

Thank you, Paulina!

e did it!

PiRATES could return at any time," Pam reminded us.

"Right. Once those pirates realize they've been tricked, they won't be in a good mood," Nicky said.

"We should HURRY," the Golden Fish agreed.

"By the way, how did you get the pirates to leave the cove?" Will asked.

The Thea Sisters told their story as we swam quickly through the underground labyrinth back into the cove.

"Where are you all headed?" the Golden Fish asked us.

"To the MOVING DUNE," I replied. "Do you know it?"

"Of course! That's where I lived before I was captured," the fish replied.

"Then we are twice as lucky that we

met you," Paulina said.

"Why are you going there?" asked the fish.

"We're looking for someone," said Colette. "A **THIEF**, actually."

The Golden Fish looked surprised. "A thief? You mean, like the pirates?"

"We asked the pirates about the *Sea Violin*," Will informed everyone.

"But they didn't seem to know anything about it, and I *believe* them," I added.

I will be your guide!

The fish's eyes got wide. "Someone **stole** the Sea Violin? Why, that's terrible!"

Paulina nodded. "Yes, it is. Without

its MUSIC, this land will fade away forever."

"I know," said the fish sadly. "Let me be your *guide* to the Moving Dune. I will take you to the lord of the area — the COBALT HERMIT CRAB."

"A **BLUE** hermit crab?" asked Violet.

The fish nodded. "He's not the *nicest* creature in the sea, but he might be able to help you," he said.

"Thank you, Golden Fish!" I said. "Time is running out, and the FUTURE OF AQUAMARINA is at stake."

"We must all be brave," the fish said. "There is a lot of OCEAN to cross before we reach the Moving Dune. Follow me!"

THE LORD OF THE MOVING DUNE

"Do you think the Black Claw Crew will **FOLLOW** us all the way to the Moving Dune?" Paulina asked the Golden Fish.

"No — it's **BEYOND** their territory," answered the fish. "They never venture into this area for fear of the Cobalt Hermit Crab."

"Wait, you mean pirates are afraid of this crab?" Pam asked. "He sounds **SCARY**."

"He can be, but you all seem very courageous to me," the fish told her. "We'll be there soon. The **MOVING DUNE** is just past that cluster of rocks."

We swam past the rocks, and a marvemouse landscape appeared before our eyes.

"How beautiful!" Nicky cried.

"Yes. It's my home and I love it very much," said the fish.

"What is that **BIG SHELL**?" asked Colette, pointing to a shell as large as a small house.

"That is the **Seashell Palace**, home of the Cobalt Hermit Crab," he answered. "We're just about there."

We swam toward the big shell. As we got closer, we saw that the surface was **smooth** and shiny. Light glowed through round windows.

The Golden Fish opened the gate and motioned for us to proceed. We passed through a garden and entered the house. Inside, we saw piles of seashells in different shapes, sizes, and **colors**.

"The Cobalt Hermit Crab adores seashells,"

explained the fish. "He COLLECTS every one that he finds."

"They're pretty, but it's kind of a MESS in here," remarked Violet.

"Yes," Colette agreed. "He really should be more organized."

"Follow me. His rooms are this way," the Golden Fish instructed.

We traveled through the seashell, which had many small rooms. Finally, we arrived in a grand room filled with more piles of seashells — and one big, BLUE hermit crab with a bright BLUE shell.

"Good day, my lord," the Golden Fish said politely.

The hermit crab stared at the fish with beady black eyes. "Golden Fish, it's you! Where have you been hiding?"

"I was CAPTURED by the Black Claw

Crew, but these friends saved me," he explained, motioning to us.

What do you want?

The hermit crab looked at us **curiously**. "Thank you," he said.

"It was our pleasure to help the Golden Fish," Will replied.

"I see," said the hermit crab. "And now I suppose you want a **reward**?"

"It's not like that –" Will started to explain, but the hermit crab interrupted him.

"Of course it is!" he snapped. "Everything has a price."

"We were on our way to **SEE** you when we met the Golden Fish," I said. "We need some information from you."

"What information?" the hermit crab asked.

"We are searching for a **THIEF**, and the Blue Pearl told us to look here, at the Moving Dune," I explained. "This thief has taken something very important to Aquamarina: the *Sea Violin*."

"You scem very **wise**, my lord," said Will. "Surely you can help us."

The Cobalt Hermit Crab was **silent** for a moment. Then he looked right at us.

"It's true. Someone here at the **MOVING DUNE** has taken the Sea Violin."

"Then you know who it is?" Colette asked. He nodded.

"I DO KNOW. IT WAS ME!"

A shocked silence fell over the room.

A VERY CRANKY CRAB

We all stared at the hermit crab. Had he really just **admitted** to being the thief?

Pam spoke up first. "Maybe we didn't **understand** you correctly . . ."

"You understood perfectly," snapped the hermit crab, annoyed. "It was I who took the *Sea Violin*."

"But why?" Violet asked.

"**NONE OF YOUR BUSINESS**," the hermit crab said.

"But it is our business," I protested. "It is the business of every creature in this realm — a realm that is in danger of disappearing because of you!"

"How can you behave like this? Don't you

have a **heart**?" Violet scolded him.

"It is because of my **heart** that I stole the violin," said the crab. "And that is all that I will say. Now please **STOP** asking me about it!"

"Please calm down," I said. "We won't ask about your motives anymore. But you must understand that the realm is in **great danger**. Can you please give the *violin* back to us?"

Calm down . . .

Stop asking questions!

"I'm afraid that's not **POSSIBLE**," the crab replied.

"Why not?" Pam asked.

"Because the *Sea Violin* isn't here. At least, not all of it," he said.

"What do you mean?" Nicky asked.

"See for yourself," the hermit crab replied with a **MYSTERIOUS** smile. He pointed to a **mother-of-pearl** trunk at the back of the room. We rushed to open it, and as soon as we lifted the heavy lid, we saw the seashell body of the Sea Violin. It was wrapped in a piece of fine **silk**.

Violet picked it up and carefully unwrapped it. "It has no strings!" she cried. "It can't play the Music of the Sea!"

"**You did this!**" Colette squeaked angrily at the crab.

He motioned for us to follow him. He led us up a **narrow** spiral staircase and then out onto a terrace on top of the Royal Seashell.

"As you have seen, the body of the violin is here, **safe and sound**," he said. "However, the four strings have been hidden in different parts of the realm."

"**You separated them on purpose!**" Pam cried.

"Of course. It was the only way I could guarantee never having to hear the violin played again," he said.

"But that has put the realm in **TERRIBLE DANGER!**" I reminded him.

The hermit crab considered this. "Very well. I will give you the violin if you can retrieve all four strings," he said. Then he

chuckled.

"What's so *funny*?" Pam asked.

"It will not be **easy** to take the strings from their guardians," the crab replied. "The first can be found in the cave of **SALEDOR**, a fearsome dragon."

"**A DRAGON!** Squeak!" Pam cried.

"The second string is in Sirens' Bay, home of the **Emerald Sirens**," the hermit crab continued.

"They sound less **SCARY** than a dragon," Nicky remarked.

"Only in appearance," the Golden Fish chimed in. "The Emerald Sirens will **IMPRISON** anyone who listens to their magical song."

"Then we must be just as careful of them," I said.

The hermit crab continued. "The third string is located in the Sludge Pits, home of **Calamario**. He's a very unpleasant giant squid."

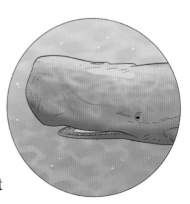

The Golden Fish nodded. "That's true!"

"And the final string is guarded by **COLOSSUS**, a huge whale," the hermit crab explained. "The string is kept inside her **gigantic** belly!"

"Colossus is *truly* massive," agreed the Golden Fish. "No creature that has been swept into her mouth has ever escaped."

"So we've got to face a dragon, sirens, a **NASTY** squid, and a giant whale," Colette repeated in a worried voice.

The Cobalt Hermit Crab **impatiently** clicked his claws. "You know what you must do. I have nothing further to say. If you manage to gather all four strings, I will see you here again. If not, farewell."

Then he scuttled back inside. We left his palace feeling very **discouraged**.

"I can't believe what that hermit crab did!" Colette exclaimed. "What would make him hate the MUSIC of the violin so much?"

"He's always been very cranky, but I

never thought he could do anything so terrible," said the Golden Fish. "I'm sorry."

"It's not your fault," I said. "And we're grateful to you for bringing us here. At least now we have a chance of getting the Sea Violin back to **Queen Anemone**."

"I'm afraid it won't be easy," the fish said.

"We can do it," Colette promised him. "We don't want your realm to disappear!"

"Thank you. Every **CREATURE** here will be in your debt," the fish replied.

Paulina opened the **MAP** of Aquamarina. "Let's see where we need to go."

The fish pointed out the four locations.

"But they're so far apart!" Pam cried.

"We'll have to **split up**," said Will.

"I think that might be the best solution," I agreed.

Just then a school of fish passed by. Half of

their scales were **brightly colored**, but the other half had faded.

"Those poor fish," said Violet sadly.

"This is all because of that COBALT HERMIT CRAB," said Paulina. "How could he be so **cruel**?"

"Let's not judge him too quickly," I said. "We don't really know him."

"He is a very **MYSTERIOUS** creature," the Golden Fish added. "None of us know where he came from. One day, he just appeared and started building his palace."

"The Eel of Ages also said there was a mystery surrounding him," Colette remembered.

"The **important** thing now is to find those four strings," Will reminded us.

"I'll take the **DRAGON** and the **SQUID**," I said. "Who wants to come with me?"

Pam and Violet quickly raised their paws. "We'll go!"

"Excellent!" said Will. "Then Paulina, Colette, Nicky, and I will go find the Emerald Sirens and the giant whale."

We thanked the Golden Fish for his help. Then we split into groups. Splitting up always makes me a little nervous, but I knew that our time was running out.

"Good luck!" I said to Will. "I hope we'll meet back here soon, with all four strings of the Sea Violin!"

See you soon!

Good luck . . .

You, too!

Bye!

THE WRATH OF SALEDOR

"How are we supposed to get the string back from a FIERCE DRAGON?" Violet asked as we swam toward Saledor's Cave.

"We just need to have FAITH," I told her. "We've come this far, haven't we?"

"Maybe he won't be *that* fierce," Pam said hopefully.

Soon we came to the entrance of a **dark** cave.

"This is it," said Pam. "I think I can see him inside."

We heard some odd, SHRILL noises.

"Is that music?" Violet wondered.

Then a voice thundered from inside the cave. **"WHO GOES THERE?"**

"We'd better go in," I told Pam and Violet, and we swam through a **tunnel** into the cave.

The dragon's **GREEN** eyes flashed when

How dare you!

he saw us. He turned and faced us.

"**WHAT DO YOU WANT?**" he asked.

"We've come to ask you for the string of the Sea Violin," Pam said.

"The future of this realm depends on the *Sea Violin*!" I called out. "If Queen Anemone can't play it again, Aquamarina will **disappear**."

The dragon blew a powerful SPRAY of water at us.

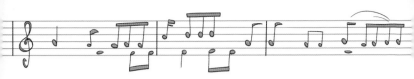

"Ahhhhh!" we shouted, ducking the blast.

"Now leave! Or **YOU'LL BE SORRY**!" Saledor threatened.

"We're not leaving without the string," Pam said bravely.

"THEN YOU SHALL FEEL MY WRATH!" the dragon cried, thrashing his long tail.

Violet jumped between Pam and Saledor. "Wait!"

"Do you dare to **challenge** me, too?" the dragon asked.

Violet looked Saledor right in the eye. "Were you playing a *violin* before?"

"What if I was?" he asked.

"Are you using the string for your violin?" Violet asked.

"It's none of your business," Saledor replied.

Violet didn't give up. "I also play the violin."

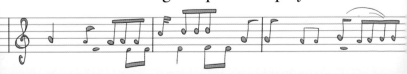

The dragon looked **interested**. "You?"

Violet nodded. "Yes. And I can **teach** you, if you like. Will you show me your instrument?"

Saledor's eyes narrowed. "I don't **trust** you!"

"I **promise** that I will be careful," Violet said, smiling. "I just want to see it."

"If you try to steal it, I shall **BLAST** you!" Saledor said.

"I know," Violet said. "That's why you can **trust** me."

The dragon seemed **satisfied** and lumbered deeper into his cave. He returned with a violin and a bow.

Violet held it. "It's a **beautiful** instrument," she said. "But the string from

the Sea Violin doesn't belong with the others. It's causing you **trouble**. If you have the original, I'll show you what I mean."

The dragon looked doubtful, but he retrieved the original string and gave it to Violet. She replaced the Sea Violin string with it and then played a SWEET MELODY.

"That was wonderful," he said. "How do you do it?"

"I'll show you," said Violet. She helped Saledor properly hold the violin and bow.

"Now give it a try," she said.

Saledor **delicately** moved the bow, and a pretty note sounded from the violin.

"It works!" he cried, pleased. "Thank you. The string from the Sea Violin is yours."

CALAMARIO OF THE SLUDGE PITS

"You were amazing, Vi!" Pam said, once we had left Saledor's cave. "Not only did you face a FIERCE dragon, but you figured out how to get the string from him!"

"Poor thing," Violet said. "He thought the string from the Sea Violin would help him play better. But now he knows."

"One string down, one to go from Calamario," I said.

"The giant squid from the Sludge Pits!" Pam remembered.

"That doesn't sound like a very nice place," Violet said.

"But how bad is a SLUDGY SQUID when you've taken down a dragon?" Pam teased.

I had entered the **location** of the Sludge Pits into my wrist computer, and I checked it.

"We need to head **NORTH**," I said.

"To the **Sludge Pits**!" Pam cheered.

After we swam for a while, we noticed that the ocean floor beneath us was no longer PALE sand. It now looked like a GREENISH, BROWNISH slush.

"Let me guess," said Pam. "We've reached the Sludge Pits."

Violet held her nose. "It **smells** terrible!"

I watched the sludge. **BUBBLES** floated up to the surface and burst, releasing a **rotten** odor.

"What kind of a squid would live in a **stinky** place like this?" Pam wondered.

After she spoke, the sludge started to bubble furiously. The pointy head of a giant squid emerged from the slime!

"Who has entered my Sludge Pits?" the squid asked, staring at us with his enormouse **Black eyes**.

"It must be Calamario!" Violet murmured.

We quickly stepped back, expecting him to lash out and ATTACK us. But Calamario just kept staring at us.

"Are you Calamario?" I asked.

Oh!

There's Calamario!

Ack!

"Yes I am," he replied. "But **WHO ARE YOU** and what do you want?"

He had fully emerged from the sludge, and his long arms were **wriggling** very close to us.

"Our names are Thea, Violet, and Pam, and we are here to ask for your **help**," I replied. "We know that the Cobalt Hermit Crab has entrusted you with one of the strings for the Sea Violin."

"That is true," Calamario replied.

"We have come to ask for the string," I continued. "Without it, Queen Anemone can no longer play the

Music of the Sea, which is causing Aquamarina to disappear. Soon it will **Fade away** forever."

"**YOU CAN'T HAVE THE STRING!**" the squid snapped.

"Why not?" Pam asked, shocked.

"Please, you must **help** save Aquamarina!" Violet pleaded.

But the squid childishly **SMACKED** his arms into the sludge, sending the **STINKY SLIME** spraying all over us.

"You are not very nice!" Violet said, wiping off her face.

"And you are **pests**," snapped the giant squid. "Now I'm going back to my nap. When I wake up again, I don't want to see you here. Understand?"

"I'm afraid not!" Pam replied.

The squid **FROZE**. "What did you say?"

"I said, we are **NOT** leaving here without the string," Pam said firmly.

Calamario pulled his entire body out of the mud and swam toward Pam. She BRAVELY stood her ground.

The squid looked at her with his **LARGE EYES**. "You have courage. This *pleases* me. So I will give you all the chance to win the string from me, if you can pass a test."

"What kind of test?" Pam asked.

"A TEST OF STRENGTH," the squid answered.

"That's not fair," Violet protested. "You

We're not leaving!

are much LARGER and STRONGER than we are!"

"We will wager the string from the Sea Violin in a TUG-OF-WAR over this sludge puddle," Calamario explained. "one of my arms against all SiX of yours."

"We can't accept," Violet whispered to me and Pam. "If we fall into the sludge, we'll be stuck."

"We can do it!" Pam said confidently. "It's three against one."

"Besides, this is our only chance to get the string," I pointed out.

I turned to Calamario. "We accept your challenge!"

The squid picked up a long rope of braided algae and gave us one end, taking the other in one of his arms.

"BEGIN!" he yelled, and we began to

pull on the rope with all of our might.

Calamario's arm was **VERY STRONG**. We held our ground. After a few minutes, though, we began to lose energy.

"Thea, he's too strong. We're going to lose this," Pam whispered to me.

"I have a plan," I said. "I'll count to three, and we'll all loosen our grip so he thinks we've given up. Then we'll give a STRONG TUG with all of our strength."

Oof!

Don't give up!

He's too strong . . .

Pam and Violet nodded, and I softly counted.

"one . . . two . . . three!"

We all stopped pulling so hard. Calamario thought he was winning, so he stopping pulling, too. Then we **yanked** the rope with all the strength we had left.

Splash! Calamario tumbled into the puddle of the sludge. **WE HAD WON!**

"Fine. The string of the Sea Violin is yours," he grumbled, climbing out to give it to us.

We accepted it, thanked him, and then swam back toward the Cobalt Hermit Crab.

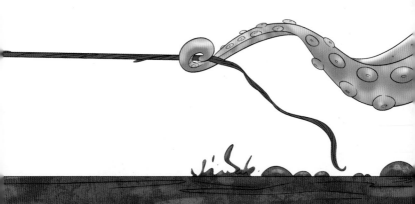

BEWARE THE
SIRENS' TRICKS!

We returned to the Moving Dune as quickly as we could, happy to have retrieved the two violin strings. At the same time, Will, Nicky, Colette, and Paulina were finally reaching their first destination, Sirens' Bay.

"I wonder what the Emerald Sirens will be like," Colette said.

"The Golden Fish made them sound very DANGEROUS," said Paulina.

"Look! I think we're here!" Nicky cried, pointing ahead.

Before them was a pretty village filled with houses decorated with colorful seashells.

"Let's approach slowly," Will said. "If they start SINGING, cover your ears!"

They swam up to two **beautiful sirens** sitting on a bench. Each had a fish tail instead of legs.

"Hello," Will said.

"Hello," replied the first siren, who was braiding her companion's long hair.

She **STUDIED** the mice. Then the other siren spoke up. "What brings you to Sirens' Bay?" she asked.

Hello . . .

"We're here to ask for your **help**, kind sirens," said Paulina.

"We're happy to help you, if we can," replied the sirens together. Their voices sounded light and musical.

Paulina continued. "We know that you are the guardians of a very precious object: a string from the Sea Violin."

The sirens looked at each other.

"Is that true?" Will asked.

"It's true, but I'm afraid you should be talking to our queen, *Esmeralda*," the blue-eyed siren informed him.

"Can you take us to her?" Nicky asked.

"Gladly!" said the siren, smiling.

The sirens led them through the village to a house that was **LARGER** and more decorated with **shells** than the others.

"Wait here, please," one of them said, and

she went inside. She returned a moment later. "The QUEEN will see you," she said.

Will, Nicky, Colette, and Paulina entered a large, circular room. Queen Esmeralda sat in the center, on a THRONE shaped like a seashell. She was stunningly beautiful, with long, blonde hair that cascaded down her back in a loose braid.

"Welcome," she greeted them sweetly with a wide smile. "Let us talk about the reason you're here. I'm told you desire the string of the Sea Violin."

"We are trying to SAVE Aquamarina," Will said.

The queen nodded. Then she opened her mouth and began to sing.

"You strangers may be sweet and kind,
But what is it you hope to find?
The Sea Violin is our greatest treasure.

Its worth is something none can measure.
How dare you ask us for this string?
Your request is far beyond daring."

Luckily, our friends remembered to **cover their ears** before Esmeralda started singing. They didn't remove their 🐾🐾🐾🐾 until they saw the queen was silent.

"I see that you don't like my song," Esmeralda said. "I was just trying to **explain** that I cannot give the string to strangers. It is too valuable."

"But we are on a **MISSION** from Queen Anemone," Nicky explained.

Esmeralda smiled. "Ah, I see. Then perhaps we can make a **TRADE**."

"What kind of trade?" Colette asked.

Esmeralda pointed at Will. "**I WANT HIM**."

"He is not an object to trade!" Paulina protested.

"Relax," said the queen. "I don't want to **keep** him. I just want to dance with him. Then you may have the string."

"May we talk among ourselves about it?" Will asked, and the queen nodded.

Our friends left the room huddled together.

"We can't accept. It's a **TRAP**," Paulina whispered.

"Exactly," said Colette. "If you're dancing with Esmeralda, you won't be able to cover your ears if she sings."

"You can use these!" Nicky said, pulling some **earplugs** from the pocket of her wet suit. "I always keep them with me when I go underwater."

"Nicky, that's perfect!" Paulina said.

Will put in the **EARPLUGS**. "I can read lips, so Esmeralda won't realize I can't hear her if she speaks to me."

They returned to the throne room. "We accept your terms, Esmeralda. I will dance with you for one song."

Esmeralda swam toward Will. "Good. You've made the right choice."

She clapped her hands, and music filled the room. Will took her in his arms and they began to dance.

Suddenly, Esmeralda frowned.

"You've tricked me!" she cried. She twirled her finger in the water and Will's earplugs magically floated out.

"That wasn't part of our deal," the queen said angrily.

"You asked for a dance, and that's what you got," Will replied.

"NEW RULES!" cried Esmeralda. "No earplugs, or you won't get the string."

Will knew that the queen might **imprison**

him. But he also knew that he had to SAVE Aquamarina.

"I'll do it," he agreed.

"**WILL, NO!**" Paulina yelled.

Will and Esmeralda danced again, and she placed her mouth close to Will's ear and sang.

Will felt himself falling under the queen's spell. Then he spotted Paulina TEARFULLY watching. He locked eyes with her. His mind suddenly felt CLEAR!

The music stopped. Esmeralda was amazed that Will had not fallen under her spell.

"Have it, then!" she said crossly. "**The string is yours!**"

COLOSSUS, WHALE OF THE DEEP

Will took the string from Queen Esmeralda and he, Nicky, Paulina, and Colette quickly swam away from Sirens' Bay.

"There is no time to rest," Will said. "Now we've got to find **COLOSSUS**, Whale of the Deep."

"That was a close one!" Colette remarked as they swam. "When Esmeralda took out your earplugs, I thought it was ALL OVER."

"I still don't understand how you didn't fall under her spell," Nicky added.

"I'm not sure, either," Will said. Then he smiled at Paulina. "But somehow I found the strength to resist her song."

"So, how do we find Colossus?" Nicky asked.

"And how do we get the string from her **belly**?" Colette added.

"Suddenly, the sirens don't seem all that SCARY," said Paulina.

Will looked at the map. "If we keep swimming this way, we should run into Colossus," he said, motioning with his paw.

The mouselets followed Will. Soon they came to an **enormouse shadow** that blocked the sunlight coming through the water. They looked up to see the underbelly of the **GIANT WHALE**!

"Colossus!" Nicky cried.

But before they could say a word to her, a *STRONG CURRENT* picked them up. It carried them right into Colossus's huge **open mouth**!

"**HEEEEEELP!**" they shouted as they were pulled down into the whale's mouth.

Nicky got to her feet. "It's **SQUISHY** in here," she said. "Kind of like a **SPONGY** cave."

Will activated the flashlight on his wrist computer. "Is everyone all right?"

"I think so," said Paulina. "Just shaken up."

"At least we don't have to worry how we're going to get **inside** the whale!" Colette joked.

The others turned on their FLASHLIGHTS, too.

"I think that's the whale's **throat**," Colette said. "See that thing hanging down?"

"It's called a uvula," said Nicky. "But what's that dangling from it?"

"It's the violin string!" Paulina cried.

Will studied it. "We can't reach it."

"What if we **CLIMB** on one another's

shoulders?" Nicky suggested.

"We need to be careful," Will warned. "We don't want the whale to cough us up before we get the string."

"Okay, let's do this!" Colette said. "I'll get on Nicky's shoulders. Then Will and Paulina, you hoist us up!"

They quickly got to work. Colette SWAYED back and forth a little as she tried to grab the string. Finally, her paw got a grip on it.

"Got it!" she cried, pulling it off the uvula.

Suddenly, Colossus had a gigantic sneeze!

Aaaaaachooooo!

The mice tumbled out of the great beast's mouth. They ended up on the whale's back as she began to rise to the surface.

For the first time since their adventure began, they were above the water. Colossus swam off, leaving our friends bouncing on top of the **churning** waves.

"Well, we've got the strings," Colette said. "But what do we do now?"

"Look!" cried Paulina, pointing.

A group of giant **GREEN SEA TURTLES** was swimming toward them. On each turtle sat a beautiful ocean fairy!

"We are the **Fairies of the Warm Sea**. We are here to help you," said a fairy with green hair. "Climb on!"

Will, Nicky, Colette, and Paulina each climbed on top of a sea turtle, **helped** by one of the fairies.

"Thank you so much!" said Colette.

"How did you find us?" asked Will.

"This is our sea," said the fairy. "We watch over the creatures who live here, and help those we find who are in **trouble**. Can we take you somewhere?"

"The **MOVING DUNE**, please," Will said.

The fairy smiled. "Very well. Hold on tight!" She directed the sea turtles **AWAY** from Colossus and toward the home of the Cobalt Hermit Crab.

Our mission was almost complete!

How nice!

You're safe!

Thanks!

Cool!

RETURN TO THE MOVING DUNE

After Pam, Violet, and I reached the Moving Dune, we **waited** for Will and the others in front of the Seashell Palace.

Time passed, and our friends didn't arrive. Although I was worried, I kept reassuring Violet and Pam that everything was fine.

Finally, we saw something swimming toward us.

"**SEA TURTLES!**" Pam cried.

"Who's that on their backs?" Violet asked.

As they got closer, we saw that they were carrying beautiful fairies — and our friends!

"You made it!" I cried. I was so happy to see them **safe and sound**.

They climbed down off the sea turtles and swam toward us.

"**Group hug!**" Pam shouted, and we all greeted one another happily.

"How did it go?" I asked.

"Great!" replied Colette. "Well, we did have a few **problems** . . ."

"But the Fairies of the Warm Sea came

Hooray!

Good to see you!

Great job!

to our rescue," finished Nicky.

"Thank you for helping our friends," I said to the fairies.

"It was a pleasure to help you," replied a green-haired fairy.

"Did you find the strings?" Pam asked.

"We have them both!" Will answered, showing them to us.

"And how about you?" Paulina asked us.

"Yes!" replied Violet, holding up the two strings we had found.

"**HOORAY!**" the Thea Sisters cheered.

"Now we just have to bring these inside and show the COBALT HERMIT CRAB that we kept up our end of the bargain," said Colette.

One of the Fairies of the Warm Sea spoke up. "We will wait for you here. Then we will take you to **Pink Pearl Castle**."

"Thank you!" we cried.

We entered the Seashell Palace and found the Cobalt Hermit Crab busy with one of his piles of shells.

"Excuse me," Will said politely.

The crab JUMPED, and he turned to look at us.

"Ah, it's you," he said.

"We brought you the four strings of the Sea Violin," Will said, showing him. "And

Here it is!

now we would like the instrument, please."

The hermit crab's eyes **bulged** with surprise. He fetched the Sea Violin from the mother-of-pearl trunk. Then he handed it to Will.

"Here it is," he said. "Now go, before I **CHANGE MY MIND**."

"Thank you for respecting our agreement," I said.

"It was foolish of me!" the crab snapped.

Poor thing . . .

"For when that violin plays, it will bring me great **unhappiness**."

"What do you mean?" Paulina asked.

But the hermit crab just turned his back to us and **STARED** at his seashells.

"We should go," Will said, motioning to us.

"I feel **sorry** for him," said Paulina as we left the palace. "He seems very sad about something."

"Yes, and his last comment was very **mysterious**," Colette said.

"I agree," I said. "But we don't have time to find out what's bothering him, I'm afraid. We must save **Aquamarina**!"

Outside the palace, the fairies were waiting for us.

"Jump on the sea turtles," a fairy told us. "We'll soon be at the **Pink Pearl Castle**!"

QUEEN ANEMONE'S MUSIC

We arrived at the Pink Pearl Castle, our hearts filled with hope. Soon we would give the Sea Violin back to Queen Anemone, and Aquamarina would be saved!

First we had to swim through the coral wall. But this time we passed through as guests, not prisoners, so we were in no danger from its STINGING BRANCHES.

"Traveling with fairies is much easier!" Pam commented.

Paulina touched her arm where it had been stung by the coral and smiled. Thanks to the Fairies of the Deep, it was fine!

The turtles stopped in front of the main entrance. We climbed off and thanked them for their help.

"Thank you for **saving** our realm," one of the fairies said.

Inside the castle, it was strangely quiet.

"I don't see a single **fairy** anywhere," Colette remarked as we walked down the long hallways lined with pink pearls.

Finally we came to Queen Anemone's **THRONE ROOM**. All the fairies of the court were there, waiting for us, and the queen was seated on her throne.

"Come forward, please," she said.

We walked past the rows of **fairies** and stopped

I don't see anyone . . .

Where are the fairies?

in front of Queen Anemone.

"I am so **happy** to see you again. We have been worried about you!" she said.

"It was a **difficult mission**," Will explained. "But we completed it."

He produced the *Sea Violin* and the four strings.

The queen smiled and rose to her feet. I could see tears in her blue eyes.

"Aquamarina is saved, thanks to you," she said, coming toward us.

Come forward, please!

Hmmm . . .

The fairies all clapped, smiling brightly.

I looked happily at the Thea Sisters and Will. What a joyful moment!

Will handed the Sea Violin and its strings to the queen. She brought it back to her throne. Working quickly and carefully, she put the strings back on the instrument.

Then she looked at the violin and smiled.

She produced a long bow made of RED coral, tucked the violin under her chin, and began to PLAY.

A beautiful melody filled the throne room. I had never heard anything like it. It was intense music, sad and happy at the same time.

As the music played, everything around us seemed to **glow** with new light and bright colors. The fairies' dresses shone in beautiful hues. Their hair became **shinier**, and their eyes brighter.

A **rainbow** appeared, arching across the throne room. It reflected off the mother-of-pearl walls and **ILLUMINATED** Queen Anemone's throne.

Then the queen stopped playing.

"Slowly, **COLOR** and **LIFE** will return to Aquamarina," she said. "And it is all thanks to you."

"We were happy to help, Your Majesty," Will said with a bow.

"However, I would like to know: Who is **responsible** for the theft?" she asked.

Before we could respond, we heard a **CLATTER** outside the throne room.

We all turned to look.

"It's the COBALT HERMIT CRAB!" cried Pam.

"What is he doing here?" asked Colette.

We held our breath as the crab entered the room.

THE MYSTERY OF
THE CRAB

We all watched as the Cobalt Hermit Crab walked up to Queen Anemone's throne, his claws clacking against the polished floor.

"Your Majesty, I beseech you," he said. "STOP PLAYING the Sea Violin!"

The queen looked puzzled. "You know I cannot do that. This music keeps our realm alive."

"And it also BREAKS MY HEART," said the hermit crab. "When I hear it, I plummet into despair! That's why I stole the Sea Violin!"

The fairies gasped.

"Silence, please," the queen told them.

"I know it was a terrible thing to do," the crab continued.

"Indeed it was," Queen Anemone agreed.

"I realized that when your friends chose to face the **DANGEROUS** quests I sent them on to find the four strings," he said.

The queen nodded. "Our friends have good hearts and have saved Aquamarina."

"And I have a **wicked** heart," said the hermit crab. "Part of me hoped they would FAIL. I ask for your forgiveness."

Hmm . . .

Forgive me!

Queen Anemone turned to us.

"What happened when you brought this hermit crab the four strings? Did he try to **trick** you or go back on his bargain?" she asked.

"No, Your Majesty," Will said. "He gave us the Sea Violin as he promised."

"But he looked **very sad**," Paulina added.

"I must go before you **play** the violin again," said the Cobalt Hermit Crab.

"I forgive you," said the queen, stepping up to him. To everyone's surprise, she placed a **kiss** on the hermit crab's head.

Suddenly, a vortex of water and fairy dust swirled through the room. When it subsided, the hermit crab was gone — and in his place was a **handsome prince**!

Queen Anemone stared into the eyes of the prince. **TEARS** ran down her cheeks.

"Nautilus! Is it really you?" she cried with joy.

Prince Nautilus held his arms out in front of him and stared at them in wonder. He touched his face. "I don't know how it's possible, but yes, **my love**, it really is me!"

Then he hugged her tightly.

"Hooray for Prince Nautilus and Queen Anemone!" the fairies rejoiced.

"What happened to you?" the queen asked Nautilus. "Where have you been all this time?"

I'll never leave you again!

"It is a *long* and **STRANGE** story," Prince Nautilus said, and we all listened intently as he told his tale.

"Right after we became engaged, I

had reason to travel across the Infinite Abyss," he began. "I know how **DANGEROUS** that place can be, but I felt fearless. I was halfway across when I felt a *DARK FORCE* coming from the deep."

I saw Violet SHUDDER. She remembered that dark pull very well.

"Without thinking, I looked down," the prince continued. "I was sucked into the abyss. A kind fish helped me return to the surface. But by then it was *TOO LATE*."

By now we were starting to understand what had happened.

"I fell victim to the **evil magic** of the abyss. I was transformed into the Cobalt Hermit Crab!" the prince explained.

"THAT'S TERRIBLE!" the queen cried.

"After I *transformed*, I lost my memory," Prince Nautilus continued. "I was adrift and alone. And every night, when you played the music of the Sea Violin, I felt terribly sad. I didn't understand why, but now I know it was because my BROKEN HEART missed you so much. I stole the Sea Violin because I couldn't bear the sadness."

"Oh, Nautilus, if only I had known it was you!" Queen Anemone cried.

Nautilus nodded to us. "These good strangers touched something in me. I did not want to see Aquamarina disappear. And then when I came here . . ."

"Our love broke the curse," the queen finished.

"Now that I've found you again, I'll never leave," he said, getting down on one knee. "Will you still be my wife?"

"YES!" she replied, and everyone cheered.

A FAIRY-TALE WEDDING

"What a **happy ending** to this adventure!" said Violet. "Not only is Aquamarina saved, but the queen has found her **lost love**."

"And we're invited to the WEDDING," said Pam. "I'm sure there'll be a great feast."

Colette was the only Thea Sister frowning. "I'm glad we're invited, but we can't wear these **wet suits** to a royal wedding," she said.

"What's wrong with them?" asked Will.

"They're fine for a mission, but this is a SPECIAL EVENT!" Colette replied.

"I wonder if the **fairies** would mind lending us some clothes?" Paulina asked.

One of the Fairies of the Deep

approached us, smiling sweetly.

"We could not help overhearing you," she said. "We would like to *invite* you to take a look at our wardrobe."

Colette perked up. "We'd love to!"

We laughed to see our friend light up with **joy** so quickly. Then we followed the fairy down a long corridor and into an enormouse circular room with a ceiling shaped like a **seashell**.

Another fairy greeted us. "I am the **royal seamstress**," she said. "Please try on anything you like. Every garment is **different**. I sewed them all myself."

We couldn't believe our eyes. The room was filled with beautiful dresses!

"This fabric is LIGHTER than silk," Colette marveled, touching a SKY-BLUE dress.

"And look at the pearls on this YELLOW gown," said Pam.

"I found the prettiest GREEN

Fabumouse!

Gorgeous!

slippers to go with this green gown!" said Nicky.

It was difficult to **decide** what to wear, but in the end, the fairies helped us each choose the *perfect* gown.

"I feel like a real princess," Violet said, **twirling** around in a long purple dress embroidered with stars.

"I know what you mean," agreed Paulina

I chose the green one!

I love the aqua . . .

Yellow for me!

as she clipped a blue star into her hair. "It's like we're all part of the fairy tale!"

"You look fabumouse, Thea!" Pam said.

I smiled. "Thank you." I did feel very elegant in my blue silk gown.

The Fairies of the Deep even did our hair for us! Thanks to them, we all looked wonderful when it came time for the wedding. The fairies led us through the castle

to the Grand Ballroom, which was filled with fairies in **gorgeous** gowns. Will came over, wearing a pearl-gray suit.

"You all look GREAT!" he told us.

"I see you've cleaned up, too," I said.

"Now do you understand why we couldn't wear our **wet suits** here?" Colette asked, motioning to the other wedding guests.

Suddenly, a blaring TRUMPET filled the room. Everyone stopped talking and turned to the main door.

Queen Anemone walked in. She looked stunning, wearing a pale pink gown decorated with seashells and pearls. A tiara sparkled on top of her head.

"What a dress!" said Colette.

Then Nautilus stepped in, wearing a suit with a **mother-of-pearl** sheen. He took Anemone's hand and they walked through the ballroom together.

"They look so happy!" Violet said.

The couple stopped in front of a large seashell.

"That shell is filled with sand from all over the realm," a nearby fairy explained.

A fairy with a bushy WHITE BEARD and a fish tail officiated the ceremony. When he tapped his scepter on the ground, Anemone and Nautilus each took a HANDFUL of sand. Then they clasped hands, combining the sand, and shared a kiss.

A cheer went up from the crowd, and fairies started blowing BUBBLES that floated all over the ballroom.

"Hooray for Queen Anemone and Prince Nautilus!" everyone cheered.

Then the celebration began.

THE GOLDEN SEA HORSES

When the ceremony was over, the wedding celebration began. The musicians struck up a sweet, romantic tune and the crowd parted for Anemone and Nautilus. It was time for the first dance!

The queen and her prince gazed into each other's eyes as they twirled around.

"They're so graceful, it's like they're floating," Colette remarked.

"All you have to do is look into their eyes to see how in love they are," added Violet.

It was a beautiful sight. Above the dancers, golden garlands hung from the ceiling, along with ribbons adorned with shells and sea flowers.

The first SONG ended, and the musicians struck up another tune. Fairy couples joined Anemone and Nautilus on the dance floor.

Will turned to Paulina. "May I have this dance?" he asked, holding out his paw.

"Of course!" Paulina replied. She put her paw in his, and he led her out onto the dance floor.

The other Thea Sisters and I watched as Will and Paulina twirled across the Grand Ballroom.

"They look so sweet," Colette said.

"Speaking of sweets," said Pam. "When

Dance with me?

Yes!

do we get to eat some WEDDING CAKE?"

We all laughed.

"I don't know if it's time for cake yet, but there's a pretty nice spread over there," Nicky said, nodding toward the wall.

Long tables were PILED with delicious-looking food. We walked over to try some.

"They're all desserts!" Pam cried happily.

Each one we tried was more delicious than the next. Almond cookies with coral-colored icing. Pastries shaped like seashells. Tarts with jewel-colored fruit.

Then the musicians stopped playing, and two fairies came in carrying the WEDDING CAKE. It had three tiers, with turquoise icing and sugar decorations shaped like coral, starfish, and seashells.

Queen Anemone and Prince Nautilus

walked up to the cake, hand in hand, and cut the first slice.

The room erupted in CHEERS for the newlyweds. The music started up again and they danced away while fairies cut the rest of the cake.

"This is the BEST WEDDING ever!"

How romantic!

What a cake!

Yummy!

My love . . .

said Pam, taking a bite of her piece.

The **celebration** continued with more dancing, food, and laughter.

Queen Anemone and Prince Nautilus approached us. They both looked so happy.

"**Thank you** all for taking part in this celebration," the queen said.

"I must thank you as well," said Nautilus. "Without you I would not have found my **true love** again. And I would still be a hermit crab!"

"Even as a **HeRmit CRaB**, you came to the palace and asked for forgiveness," I reminded him. "Your **good heart** won the day, in the end."

Nautilus smiled. "That is kind of you," he said, and then he raised his glass. "May **peace** and **love** rule this world forever!"

We all cheered.

"And now I am sorry to say that we must leave," Will said.

Our time in **Aquamarina** had flown by!

"We understand," said Queen Anemone. "You will be our honored guests any time you return."

"Thank you, Your Majesty," I said.

"You are welcome," said the queen. "The **PASSAGE** between Aquamarina and your

Thank you!

Good-bye!

The passage is open . . .

world is still open. But you must go quickly. The Golden Sea Horses will take you to the Bridge of Worlds."

Hey!

They're so cute!

We all said **farewell** and left to change back into our wet suits. Fairy attendants brought us to the Golden Sea Horses.

"They're such GORGEOUS creatures!" Nicky exclaimed.

"It's a shame we have to leave," Violet said with a sigh. "Now that the *Music of the Sea* is playing again, this world has become even more beautiful."

She was right. As the sea horses took us

away from the palace, we passed many fish. Their **bright colors** had returned.

The Golden Sea Horses *SWIFTLY* carried us across the realm. It wasn't long before we saw a large **STONE BRIDGE** arching up from the ocean floor and rising above the water's surface.

We climbed off the sea horses and thanked them for the ride.

"I'll **miss** this place," Colette said sadly.

"We all will," I agreed. "But we'll always keep the memories we made here in our **hearts**."

"Come on!" Will said, climbing up the steps of the **BRIDGE**. "There should be an agent waiting for us!"

And so with one last **LOOK** back, we left Aquamarina.

THE MUSIC OF
THE SEA

As we emerged into the sunlight, we saw a helicopter hovering above us.

"As punctual as ever!" said Will, pleased.

The helicopter silently sank down toward us. A rope ladder unfurled and we all climbed aboard.

Then the helicopter flew back up into the sky and headed toward the horizon. When we looked down, the bridge had disappeared beneath the waves. The passage to the world of Aquamarina had closed.

"We'll drop you off at Mouseford Academy, but I must continue directly to the **SEVEN ROSES UNIT**," Will explained. "I wish I could stay and visit, but I'm anxious to get back and look at the data we collected."

"We understand," I said. "And if you need any **help**, you know where to find us."

"Thanks, Thea," he said. "And I also want to compliment you all. You demonstrated **courage** and **skill** on this risky mission. But I knew you would!"

"Thanks, Will!" the Thea Sisters replied.

By now we could see Whale Island on the

First stop, Mouseford!

horizon. The sky was turning **RED** as the sun set behind the academy.

The helicopter landed. We said good-bye to Will and jumped down to the ground, and the helicopter quickly flew off.

"Should we go to the **beach** and enjoy this **sunset**?" I asked the Thea Sisters.

"Yes!" they replied.

So we took a walk down to the *sandy* beach and gazed out at the *peaceful* ocean. All of our thoughts immediately returned to Aquamarina.

"Can you hear the waves lapping against the shore?" Violet asked. "It reminds me of the *Music of the Sea*!"

We listened to the music of the waves as the *sun* disappeared below the horizon and into the sea.

"I can almost imagine the sun setting on

Pink Pearl Castle," said Colette.

"Helping **Aquamarina** was such a fun mission," Nicky remarked.

"You said it!" Pam agreed.

Violet nodded. "I'm already looking forward to our next adventure!"

Paulina smiled. "If I know Will Mystery, we won't have to wait very long for it!"

Don't miss any of my fabumouse special editions!

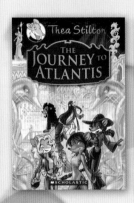

THE JOURNEY
TO ATLANTIS

THE SECRET OF
THE FAIRIES

THE SECRET OF
THE SNOW

THE CLOUD
CASTLE

THE TREASURE
OF THE SEA

Don't miss any of these exciting Thea Sisters adventures!

Thea Stilton and the Dragon's Code

Thea Stilton and the Mountain of Fire

Thea Stilton and the Ghost of the Shipwreck

Thea Stilton and the Secret City

Thea Stilton and the Mystery in Paris

Thea Stilton and the Cherry Blossom Adventure

Thea Stilton and the Star Castaways

Thea Stilton: Big Trouble in the Big Apple

Thea Stilton and the Ice Treasure

Thea Stilton and the Secret of the Old Castle

Thea Stilton and the Blue Scarab Hunt

Thea Stilton and the Prince's Emerald

Thea Stilton and the Mystery on the Orient Express

Thea Stilton and the Dancing Shadows

Thea Stilton and the Legend of the Fire Flowers

Thea Stilton and the Spanish Dance Mission

Thea Stilton and the Journey to the Lion's Den

Thea Stilton and the Great Tulip Heist

Thea Stilton and the Chocolate Sabotage

Thea Stilton and the Missing Myth

Thea Stilton and the Lost Letters

Thea Stilton and the Tropical Treasure

Thea Stilton and the Hollywood Hoax

Thea Stilton and the Madagascar Madness

Don't miss any of my adventures in the Kingdom of Fantasy!

THE KINGDOM OF FANTASY

THE QUEST FOR PARADISE:
THE RETURN TO THE KINGDOM OF FANTASY

THE AMAZING VOYAGE:
THE THIRD ADVENTURE IN THE KINGDOM OF FANTASY

THE DRAGON PROPHECY:
THE FOURTH ADVENTURE IN THE KINGDOM OF FANTASY

THE VOLCANO OF FIRE:
THE FIFTH ADVENTURE IN THE KINGDOM OF FANTASY

THE SEARCH FOR TREASURE:
THE SIXTH ADVENTURE IN THE KINGDOM OF FANTASY

THE ENCHANTED CHARMS:
THE SEVENTH ADVENTURE IN THE KINGDOM OF FANTASY

THE PHOENIX OF DESTINY:
AN EPIC KINGDOM OF FANTASY ADVENTURE

THE HOUR OF MAGIC:
THE EIGHTH ADVENTURE IN THE KINGDOM OF FANTASY

THE WIZARD'S WAND:
THE NINTH ADVENTURE IN THE KINGDOM OF FANTASY

Be sure to read all my fabumouse adventures!

#1 Lost Treasure of the Emerald Eye

#2 The Curse of the Cheese Pyramid

#3 Cat and Mouse in a Haunted House

#4 I'm Too Fond of My Fur!

#5 Four Mice Deep in the Jungle

#6 Paws Off, Cheddarface!

#7 Red Pizzas for a Blue Count

#8 Attack of the Bandit Cats

#9 A Fabumouse Vacation for Geronimo

#10 All Because of a Cup of Coffee

#11 It's Halloween, You 'Fraidy Mouse!

#12 Merry Christmas, Geronimo!

#13 The Phantom of the Subway

#14 The Temple of the Ruby of Fire

#15 The Mona Mousa Code

#16 A Cheese-Colored Camper

#17 Watch Your Whiskers, Stilton!

#18 Shipwreck on the Pirate Islands

#19 My Name Is Stilton, Geronimo Stilton

#20 Surf's Up, Geronimo!

#21 The Wild, Wild West

#22 The Secret of Cacklefur Castle

A Christmas Tale

#23 Valentine's Day Disaster

#24 Field Trip to Niagara Falls

#25 The Search for Sunken Treasure

#26 The Mummy with No Name

#27 The Christmas Toy Factory

#28 Wedding Crasher

#29 Down and Out Down Under

#30 The Mouse Island Marathon

#31 The Mysterious Cheese Thief

Christmas Catastrophe

#32 Valley of the Giant Skeletons

#33 Geronimo and the Gold Medal Mystery

#34 Geronimo Stilton, Secret Agent

#35 A Very Merry Christmas

#36 Geronimo's Valentine

#37 The Race Across America

#38 A Fabumouse School Adventure

#39 Singing Sensation

#40 The Karate Mouse

#41 Mighty Mount Kilimanjaro

#42 The Peculiar Pumpkin Thief

#43 I'm Not a Supermouse!

#44 The Giant Diamond Robbery

#45 Save the White Whale!

#46 The Haunted Castle

#47 Run for the Hills, Geronimo!

#48 The Mystery in Venice

#49 The Way of the Samurai

#50 This Hotel Is Haunted!

#51 The Enormouse Pearl Heist

#52 Mouse in Space!

#53 Rumble in the Jungle

#54 Get into Gear, Stilton!

#55 The Golden Statue Plot

#56 Flight of the Red Bandit

The Hunt for the Golden Book

#57 The Stinky Cheese Vacation

#58 The Super Chef Contest

#59 Welcome to Moldy Manor

The Hunt for the Curious Cheese

#60 The Treasure of Easter Island

#61 Mouse House Hunter

#62 Mouse Overboard!

The Hunt for the Secret Papyrus

#63 The Cheese Experiment

#64 Magical Mission